An excerpt from
The Edge of the Earth

He glanced around, then looked back at her in obvious confusion. "Are you Charlie Rowe, by any chance?" he asked in briskly accented English.

Charlotte dropped her suitcases and shoulder bag with a thump. "I'm Charlotte, not Charlie. Charlotte Rowe." She fished in her coat pocket for the photo. "I'm supposed to meet..." She stared down at the man in the picture, then back at the man before her. She said the name she knew by heart. "Dr. William Mayfair?"

His blue eyes narrowed and grew dark. "Yeah. That's me."

Charlotte stood frozen, trying to process this shocking revelation. *He* was Dr. William Mayfair, esteemed linguist and MacArthur fellow? The hottie in the cargo shorts? Dr. Mayfair wasn't an old man, not even close, and he definitely didn't look like someone who spent a lot of time in libraries. He also didn't look happy to see her. They stared at each other in awkward silence until her genteel southern breeding took over and she offered her hand.

"Hi. It's nice to meet you."

He shook it brusquely. "Hello. Welcome to Adygea."

"You look nothing like the picture."

"What picture?"

She held out the photo, realizing now that light blond hair might look a lot like gray hair if that's what you expected. Dr. Mayfair glared at it, his lips pursed tight.

"You're right. It doesn't look much like me, but I'm guessing that was by design, *Charlie*," he said, handing the photo back.

"Charlotte."

"Exactly.

Copyright 2012 Molly Joseph/Scarlet Rose Press

Cover design by Robin Ludwig Design Inc.,
http://www.gobookcoverdesign.com/

* * * * *

This book is a work of fiction. Names, characters, places, and incidents are products of the author's imagination or are used fictitiously. Any resemblance to actual events, locales, or persons living or dead, is entirely coincidental.

All characters depicted in this work of fiction are 18 years of age or older.

The Edge of the Earth

of the

Earth

By

Molly Joseph

Erotic romance by Annabel Joseph (Molly's kinky counterpart)

Mercy
Cait and the Devil
Firebird
Deep in the Woods
Fortune
Owning Wednesday
Lily Mine
Comfort Object
Caressa's Knees
Odalisque
Cirque du Minuit
Burn For You

Erotica by Annabel Joseph

Club Mephisto
Molly's Lips: Club Mephisto Retold

Coming soon:

Command Performance
Disciplining the Duchess

*This book is dedicated
with much gratitude
to my beta reader J. Luna Scuro,
for invaluable advice*

Chapter One: Something Important

Charlotte Rowe surveyed the spacious, organized suburban home, her narrowed hazel eyes missing no detail. "Roger—the serenity candles on the kitchen island. They aren't perfectly symmetrical."

She pronounced her assistant's name *Ro-zhay* the way he preferred, even though she knew he was from Buffalo and not remotely French. She'd do anything to keep him working for her. The tall, dark-haired man crossed to the candle arrangement, fiddled with the pillar on the left, and turned to look at her. "Better?"

"Just a smidge more."

He inched it over a tiny degree.

"Close. One more little hair."

Roger rolled his eyes and inched the candle an infinitesimal degree left. "Happy now, you psychopath?"

"These people hired me to transform their home into a utopia of organization. This is what they pay me for. Perfection. Attention to detail. When they return from their Hawaiian getaway, they're going to find their cluttered hellhole transformed into a showplace. And the damn candle arrangement is going to be symmetrical."

"I've said this before and I'll say it again: You have problems. Deep-seated problems." He crossed to stand by her at the door, tugging a lock of her long and slightly wild honey-brown hair. "I love you though, boss. Truly, madly, deeply. Are you ready to get out of here?"

The job was done. The photos taken, explicit directions left in each room regarding her methods of organization and ways to maximize the space she'd freed up. It had been a two-week job, the type of transformation she knew would greatly benefit the mom and dad and their three messy kids—as long as they didn't fall back into their old disorganized ways. All the clutter she'd cleared out, all the dust and drawers full of years of accumulated junk...

Roger was doing his best to nudge her out the door. "All right. Say goodbye to this one. Job's over."

"Yeah." She took a shaky breath. "It's a beautiful house, isn't it?"

"You did great work. It was a huge job and you knocked it out of the park. Now it's time to go home and put your feet up." He pried the key from her hand and locked up. He'd return it to the client when they got back from their vacation. Roger did all those little kinds of things for her, freeing up her time to do what she did best.

Oh, but it was such a magnificent house. She turned when she was almost to her car, seized with anxiety. "They won't take care of it," she said. "They'll come home from their vacation and drop their suitcases and laundry everywhere. The kids will run upstairs and pull out all those toys and—"

Roger took her face between his hands. "Look in my eyes and repeat after me. This is not my house. I'm only the organizer."

"This is not my house. I'm only the organizer."

"I have no actual control over the people in this house continuing to keep it organized."

"I have no actual control—over the people in this house—oh, Roger, I worked for hours on those toys. It took almost a whole day."

"And you were paid handsomely for your time and effort. Now those toys are no longer your problem."

The stern note in his voice went unheeded. "I labeled everything. I special-ordered those bins so they'd fit just right on those shelves, and arranged all the toys by theme. Those kids are going to completely disregard the system, I know it."

"Someday you're going to have kids, and they're going to be germy and messy and disorganized and you know what? You're going to adore them anyway."

Charlotte shook her head. "No, no kids ever. They don't respect the power of the bin."

"Your bin thing haunts me in my quieter moments."

"But—"

"Hush."

"But—"

"I will force you into treatment if you don't stop right now."

"Okay." Charlotte opened her hands from their fists and heaved a deep breath. "Okay, you're so right. Just having an organizer moment."

He arched a brow. "An organizer moment? When's the last time you took a vacation, Charlotte?"

"All my time goes to the business. New businesses are the most vulnerable to failure."

"OrganizeNation isn't a new business anymore. It's a five-year-old, thriving business, and you have employees, like *moi*, who could manage things should you take a much-needed break."

"I don't need a break." Charlotte unlocked her sedan and reached for the handle, but Roger leaned against the door, preventing her from opening it. He gave her a long, hard look.

"Answer me something, boss lady. When's the last time you got good and drunk? When's the last time you got laid, for that matter?"

Charlotte wanted to shoot back a withering response, but she couldn't. It had been...five years. She hadn't partied or had a steady boyfriend since she started her business, but she could never admit that to Roger. Five years!

Charlotte allowed herself a moment to admire her very attractive— and very gay—assistant's assets. Long, strong legs, broad shoulders, lustrous dark auburn hair. He looked fine in the tailored slacks he favored, but in jeans... God, it was enough to make a woman cry. And Roger wasn't just hot as hell. He was sweet and dependable too, unlike the cads she'd fallen in love with before she gave up dating altogether. She knew Roger led a fun, fulfilling life with his boyfriend of nearly four years. She wasn't jealous.

Oh God, yes. Yes, she was. There was Roger with his perfect relationship and life, then there was her. Boring, lonely Charlotte.

"Okay, sure," she admitted. "I could probably use a stiff drink."

"Or a stiff—"

"Roger! Thank you. Your opinion is noted."

"Come out with me tonight. I'll call Perry and he can meet us at Morrissey's. Or the KC. Any bar you want."

"So I can watch the two of you play kissyface, and listen to more lectures about how I need to get a life? No thanks. Anyway, I actually have a life tonight." She bent down to silence the notification chime on her smart phone. "Remember when I registered to volunteer at the International Center? You know, the last time you badgered me about having no life?"

"Oh, yeah. Because you speak Apache."

"Adyghe."

"An Apache finally showed up? Didn't you register there years ago?"

"Yes. So you see, this might be my one and only chance to flaunt my Adyghe-speaking skills for the aid of my fellow man. He is a man, by the way," Charlotte said, waggling her eyebrows.

"For God's sake, then. Don't let me hold you up." Roger stood back to open her car door. "Is he hot?"

It was the same question she'd been wondering about for the past two days. "I haven't met him yet. The center set up the appointment."

"Native Americans are sexy."

"Roger, it's *Adyghe*, not Apache. It's spoken in the Republic of Adygea, which is over by Russia and Turkey."

"Fine, but I stand by my comment about Native Americans. Speaking of Turkey, I guess I'd better get home and think about what to make for dinner, since you're laming out on drinks with me and Perry."

Charlotte laughed as her assistant crossed to his car, a small economy coupe. She needed to give the man another raise. Without him she'd be truly and literally sunk, especially now that OrganizeNation was expanding from Savannah to several other southern cities. Flagging social life aside, Charlotte felt like the luckiest person on the planet. She got to do what she loved for a living while making alarmingly good money at it. If only her life outside of work wasn't so depressing.

Charlotte put her business—and the fate of her most recently organized house—out of her mind as she made the short drive over to the International Services Center, a non-profit group that provided language and legal help to foreign residents of the city. She was excited at the prospect of meeting an Adyghe speaker because she'd really enjoyed speaking the language with her grandfather before he died. It had been their special way of communicating, and now that he was gone she missed the sound of it and the feel of it on her tongue. Her parents had never learned the language, and Charlotte was afraid of forgetting it, so she spoke it to herself sometimes. She sang songs her grandfather had sung her as a young child, repeated rhymes and lullabies in the quiet of her room at night. If this man she was meeting was a native speaker, she would likely talk his ear off from excitement. If he was handsome, all the better.

When she arrived, she checked in at the front desk and was directed to a wizened, gray-haired man in the corner of the lobby. So much for her daydreams of a tall, dark Caucasus stranger. The old man clutched a worn briefcase as he struggled to his feet.

"Please, Dr. Petrenko," Charlotte said in Adyghe. "Don't get up."

He looked confused—confused enough that Charlotte lapsed into English as she sat down beside him. "I'm Charlotte Rowe. Are you the one who needed an Adyghe translator?"

"You are Charlotte Rowe?"

He looked somewhat incredulous as he sidled closer. She gazed over into rheumy yet incisive eyes.

"I am sorry," he stammered, seeming to recollect himself. "My English is not so good. I search for Adyghe speaker, yes. But you speak just now...Adyghe?"

"Yes, my grandfather taught it to me. We spoke it all the time. He died a few years ago."

"He was from Adygea?"

"No, he learned it from his parents. A branch of my family came from there some generations ago."

He studied her face intently. He seemed so kind and non-threatening Charlotte couldn't feel alarmed, even when he turned and started rooting around in his overstuffed briefcase, dropping papers on the floor. She reached down to help collect them.

"Miss Rowe," he said, taking the papers. "I am a researcher, and I need a translator. But the Adyghe you speak is not the Adyghe I know."

"Oh, I'm sorry." How horribly embarrassing. "I only know what my grandfather taught me. We spoke it together for years, and he said it was Adyghe." She shrugged, feeling a flush burn across her cheeks.

"There are dialects." Dr. Petrenko's voice shook. "Many, many dialects. I search for months now to find—well. Please." The old man thrust a wrinkled page in front of her face. "Is it possible, can you read this text? I beg you, please try."

Charlotte took the paper, already dreading having to disappoint him. She squinted at the writing, expecting to see something incomprehensible. But...

"This language, can you understand it?" His tone was urgent, almost fearful.

"Yes, this is the language my grandfather taught me." She read some of the words, translating them into English. "Nasra...that has to be a name. Nasra said—or maybe replied—'You smile and pretend benevolence, but you are not so. You have taken away our fire and left us to suffer cold.' Perhaps 'bitter cold,'" she amended, considering the *buzhe* prefix.

Petrenko grasped her hand, his face transformed from anxiety to bliss. "You can never understand how glad this makes me. Read more, please."

She read the rest of the passage about a warrior, Nasra, arguing with a god named Paqa. The elderly researcher hung on every word until she reached the end of the page, with Paqa snatching some enormous, bloodthirsty eagle from the sky. She looked up at him with a smile. "Then what happens?"

Dr. Petrenko stared back at her. "I don't know yet. You must tell me. I have searched for native speakers many months but none knows this dialect. No one until you."

"Why? Is it very rare?"

"Rare, and very old. You see," he said, leaning closer, "my partner and I, we are linguists. We try to save languages. So many languages dying in small towns and villages. Half the languages of the world, *poufi*." He waved a hand. "They disappear. We find this document in Adygea. A chance finding, old Circassian text. You can translate for us." He made a gleeful sound.

"I would be happy to translate it for you. If you email me the rest of it—"

He shook his head. "Email? No. I have only this small section transcribed. The book is centuries old. To copy it is to destroy it and the town governors forbid any...how do you say..."

"They won't let you scan it? Photograph it?"

"No. And they will not allow us to move it anywhere else. There is a sad history of exploitation in this area. Cultural theft and feuding republics." He waved his hands in frustration.

Charlotte frowned. Feuding republics? "Where is the document? Who owns it?"

"It is in a rural town called Aleronsk, in Adygea. They deny the document to leave. They say if we wish to study, we are welcome. But they cannot translate. We cannot translate. *You* can." He gave her a pleading look. "You must go there. So much manuscript, hundreds of years old. You must help."

The Edge of the Earth

Charlotte shook her head. "I have a job. I run a business here. I can't just fly off to Adygea."

"But you must. At once!" The old man looked like he might cry. "You see, there is no time. This area is in turmoil. This document will not stay. You must go now, in all haste."

"The area is in turmoil? What kind of turmoil?"

Dr. Petrenko looked away, waving his hand again. "It is these republics. They are always fighting. I do not trust this document to be kept safe. The villages feud. The law is not dependable."

"And you want me to go there?"

"If you have U.S. passport, you are safe as a baby. You must go, I beg you. I promise my partner I find someone who knows this language. And it is adventure for you, no?"

Adventure. An hour ago, she'd been bemoaning the boredom of her life. But to leave her job and fly halfway across the world to some unstable Caucasus republic? "Dr. Petrenko...I don't know."

"Please, I am desperate. I look everywhere. In Adygea, Russia, Turkey, Jordan, Syria. I visit many language centers in Europe and the U.S. I study emigration records and fly to many cities. No one knows this dialect. You are the first one that reads it and understands. It is a long text, and the meaning...it can be anything. In those days they did not write down insignificant things. They only put important documents to page, you see? Very important. With your help, and this document, the language remains alive. Forever alive for research, for scholars. Please, you must come."

"Well..." Charlotte waffled, not wishing to hurt the old man with an outright refusal. "Can I think about it and let you know?"

"You must let me know soon. In a few days. My partner is there waiting for help translating. He tries to protect the document but the government there is not in support." He took her hand, gripping it surprisingly hard for a frail old man. "They think of other matters, not history and language. Miss Rowe, I beg you. My colleague—he begs—"

Charlotte extricated her hand as gently as she could. "I understand your situation, Dr. Petrenko. But I need some time to think about it. I'll let you know."

* * * * *

For the next couple days, Charlotte looked into the Republic of Adygea. Dr. Petrenko hadn't lied. The area was far from stable, but at the same time, it wasn't on the cusp of war. If it was anywhere else, she probably wouldn't have considered it, but this was her ancestors' homeland.

She told Roger about the whole situation on the phone. He insisted she should go, that he could handle the business while she was away for a few weeks. He made a good case for opportunity and adventure, droning on in his stern, gay-friend-knows-best voice. While Charlotte listened, she organized the little word tiles on her refrigerator into neat rows. In the center, she lined up four words and came a little closer to a decision.

I AM SO BORED

She was so bored with her life. As Roger pointed out, she would likely never have a chance like this again, a chance to do something adventurous and important at the same time. A chance to visit a land so special to her grandfather, and a chance to translate what could be an important historical text.

Dr. Petrenko called at regular intervals to plead with her. He told her more about his colleague, who sounded as learned and aged as Dr. Petrenko himself. He waxed lyrical about the beauty of the area, and the rich history of the small republics clustered along the Caucasus mountain chain. Finally, Charlotte decided to talk to her parents about the idea—something she'd been putting off, because she was certain they'd be against it.

Which made her think it might be the right thing to do.

The Edge of the Earth

Her parents lived in a sprawling house at the edge of a country club. The Rowe family had made a fortune in trucking and transportation in the early 1900s, and still lived on the windfall. Charlotte had grown up in comfort, taking money for granted until she left the nest and realized not all children had nannies and maids and priceless antiques underfoot. From that point, she did everything in her power to overcome her sense of entitlement. She'd worked jobs in college even though she didn't have to, and of course, she'd started her own business rather than count on her family's wealth. She'd taken out a loan to create OrganizeNation, even though her father offered the capital to set it up. It was family money, he'd said. Why shouldn't she use it?

Because she didn't want to. They hadn't even worked for it, which seemed really unfair. Sometimes she still felt like the clueless, privileged rich girl, a feeling she hated, a feeling her parents brought out every time they got together. She chafed at their conservatism and WASPy values. Her mother, as expected, was aghast at the idea of her daughter flying off to a small Caucasus republic, even to save a dying language.

"I don't care if he begged, Charlotte. I don't want you going there. Absolutely not."

"I'm a grown woman, so I don't think you can stop me. And I have to go, don't I? If no one else can do it?"

"I can't believe that. No one else in the world knows this dialect? Only you?"

"Grandfather knew it."

"Well, I blame him for this. Why on earth he even taught you that useless language is beyond me."

"Maybe this is why he taught me. Maybe this text is really important."

Her mother threw up her hands. "Honestly, sometimes you're so whimsical. This isn't fate, this is a set up. Someone over there found out you come from a wealthy family, and as soon as you show up at this...this village or what have you, the kidnappers will grab you and fire off a ransom note to me and your father."

"Kidnappers? Oh, for God's sake."

"Don't 'for God's sake' me, young lady. Gordon, talk to her."

Her father barely glanced up from his Golf Digest magazine. "Your kidnapping would really throw a wrench in that Fourth of July charity barbeque your mom's planning."

Her mother made an impatient noise and turned away. Charlotte sat back on the sofa, refusing the sweet tea and cookies the housekeeper placed on the coffee table. She looked around her parents' finely appointed parlor. This was her cushioned little shell, her mother's idea of the perfect life. Sweet tea and chintz sofas. A flawless manicure and rigidly coiffed hair that cost two hundred dollars a visit. An endless parade of society housewife friends who were as bored and unfulfilled as her. Would Charlotte be like her some day? Brittle and vaguely dissatisfied, married to a man who took every possible opportunity to be out of the house? Would she have her own daughter? Would she be trying to fix her up with all the most boring, well-connected men in town while she swanned around planning parties and charity events?

"What is this really about?" her mother asked. "Now, you want to run off and be rebellious? Now that you're almost thirty?"

"Maybe I do. Maybe I need to."

"What about your business? Aren't you in the midst of expanding?"

"My assistant can do everything I do at this point. He can oversee the staff while I manage things remotely." They sat in silence for long moments while Charlotte toyed with a snag in the chintz. "I just want to do something."

"You have done something. You started that business of yours."

"Anyone can start a business. I want to do something important, contribute something meaningful to humanity."

"Oh, well," her mother sniffed. "In that case, how about meeting a nice man and settling down and making some grandchildren for us? What about that assistant of yours? He's handsome and you get on famously."

"Roger? For real, mama?"

"Why ever not?"

"Because...because..." If she told her mother he was gay, she would disintegrate. "Because he's taken. All the good ones are, and all the available guys suck."

"Charlotte! Really, your language."

Really, your language. She hated her mother's thick southern drawl, although she knew she was afflicted with nearly the same accent. She tugged at the chintz again, twirling the thread around her finger. She needed scissors to fix the snag. Damn, forget the scissors. Forget being perfect and responsible. She made a decision. *Adventure.* She looked up at her mother.

"I already told him I would go." A lie, but one she would rectify as soon as she left her parents' house and called Ivo Petrenko. "You and daddy will have to sit back and wait for the ransom note."

Charlotte thought she saw a hint of a smile behind her dad's golf magazine. Her mother's lips drew tight across her teeth and Charlotte knew she was terribly upset, although she didn't go so far as to cry. Adele Rowe was too well-mannered a society lady to cry in public. Instead, she frowned down her nose at her daughter.

"This isn't a joke, darling. I'm afraid you'll find that out as soon as you get there. I think you've been too sheltered."

"Yes," Charlotte nodded, in perfect agreement with her for once. "I think I have."

Chapter Two: Adventure

The little prop plane banked hard left. Charlotte clamped her lips shut to contain the moan that welled inside her. In a moment she'd heave up the roiling contents of her stomach.

Oh my God. Oh my God. Oh my God. Had she really wanted adventure? If this was adventure, she'd made a huge mistake. The plane banked sharply upward, the engines screaming from either wing. She watched as her suitcase made another slow slide along the length of the plane's aisle. The other three passengers, burly Russian men who'd boarded with her in Rostov, seemed unconcerned.

She looked out the dirty window to calm herself, trying to think of anything but her impending doom. The sky blinded her as the sun rose to its zenith. The clouds were tinged with a metallic orange glow at odds with the dank, gray-metal interior of the prop plane. Below, she saw massive, unmistakable silhouettes. Rolling, forested mountains flanked by strips of lowland and scattered lakes.

She gasped as the plane began to bump up and down violently for the twentieth time. *I'm going to die in these mountains. I could have stayed in my safe little condo, done my safe little job and organized some safe little houses and been fine.* The plane turned again, banking right, and then started down in a slow angle that increased to a terrifying lunge. Her suitcase slid down the center aisle, right into the curtained cockpit. A disembodied foot jauntily kicked it back out. Charlotte closed her eyes and braced, and prayed death would be quick. She thought of her mother and father, who would grieve for their only child, and of Ivo Petrenko who would live the rest of his days with the guilt of causing her death.

Then, with a soft bump-bump, the plane was taxiing. They were earthbound. Tires hissed and brakes squealed. The engines roared in outrage before they died down to a low hum. The plane came to an abrupt stop, tossing her wandering suitcase on its side. The Russian men unbuckled their seat belts and casually prepared to disembark. They'd barely looked up from their newspapers, while Charlotte considered herself fortunate not to have peed her pants.

With a ragged sigh, she collected her baggage and followed the other passengers down the plane's stairway. She felt a strong urge to fall to her knees and kiss the ground, an impulse only squelched by her southern-bred distaste for drawing attention to herself. In some still-functioning part of her brain, she realized she would need to fly out the same way at some point to get home.

That thought was halted and filed away for a time she was more mentally capable of dealing with it. For the moment, she squinted through the afternoon glare to locate Dr. Petrenko's colleague, Dr. Mayfair. The entire trip had been planned with such haste she wasn't sure all the dots had been connected, which freaked out the organizer in her. She hoped he'd remembered to contact his partner with her arrival time, or at least an approximation of it, since her chartered connection from Rostov had a duration time of "variable." Ivo had assured her that was normal in this region, but she wasn't looking forward to any more "variable" flights soon.

The Russian men dispersed, until she stood alone across from a low terminal. *What now, Charlotte?* She didn't even know what Dr. Mayfair looked like. All she had to go on was a photo no doubt taken by Ivo's palsied hands, of a blurry gray-haired gentleman in a dark overcoat in the snow. The only person around was a blond man in cargo shorts and a tee shirt who looked to be in his mid-thirties. Not nearly old enough to be the scholar she was supposed to meet. Even in her addled state, she noted the man was handsome. Tall and built, with beautiful blue eyes and broad shoulders. Oh...nice shoulders.

Why was he staring at her?

He glanced around, then looked back at her in obvious confusion. "Are you Charlie Rowe, by any chance?" he asked in briskly accented English.

Charlotte dropped her suitcases and shoulder bag with a thump. "I'm Charlotte, not Charlie. Charlotte Rowe." She fished in her coat pocket for the photo. "I'm supposed to meet..." She stared down at the man in the picture, then back at the man before her. She said the name she knew by heart. "Dr. William Mayfair?"

His blue eyes narrowed and grew dark. "Yeah. That's me."

Charlotte stood frozen, trying to process this shocking revelation. *He* was Dr. William Mayfair, esteemed linguist and MacArthur fellow? The hottie in the cargo shorts? Dr. Mayfair wasn't an old man, not even close, and he definitely didn't look like someone who spent a lot of time in libraries. He also didn't look happy to see her. They stared at each other in awkward silence until her genteel southern breeding took over and she offered her hand.

"Hi. It's nice to meet you."

He shook it brusquely. "Hello. Welcome to Adygea."

"You look nothing like the picture."

"What picture?"

She held out the photo, realizing now that light blond hair might look a lot like gray hair if that's what you expected. Dr. Mayfair glared at it, his lips pursed tight.

"You're right. It doesn't look much like me, but I'm guessing that was by design, *Charlie*," he said, handing the photo back.

"Charlotte."

"Exactly. Would you excuse me a moment?"

He walked a few yards away and jerked a cell phone out of his pocket. He checked the screen and walked a few yards more, then a few steps again, angling his body against the backdrop of the mountains. Another few steps forward, then back, like some bizarre line dance. He tapped at the screen and ran a hand through his tousled hair, then muttered a string of English-accented profanities interspersed with the words, "Goddamn cell reception." At last, he froze in a spot near the edge of the gravel parking lot and held the phone to his ear, giving her his back.

Well. *This* was the partner excitedly awaiting her arrival? The man who'd wanted her help so badly? He looked more disgruntled than anything, and as far from her mental image of an academic linguist as anyone could be. She looked around one last time, certain this must be a huge misunderstanding. Maybe Charlie Rowe was on the next flight.

But probably not.

Dr. Mayfair looked back at her over his shoulder, then turned around and spoke loudly and sharply into the phone in a language she didn't know. Russian, maybe? She tried not to think about how firm and strong his ass looked in his cargo shorts, because, of course, that would have been totally inappropriate. For a while, he paced back and forth along the gravelly asphalt, then he stopped and shook the phone at the sky, yelling out more foreign-sounding expletives.

"Is everything okay?" Charlotte asked.

He spun to look at her with a growl of frustration. "Welcome to the Caucasus. Majestic Land of Dropped Calls." He must have gotten Ivo back on the line then, because the streams of angry language burst forth again. Surprise on top of dissonance on top of anomaly. A few minutes before, he'd spoken to her in the most proper, clipped English, and now he ranted in Russian like a native, spitting out the deep vowels and intonations that were also present in the dialect she knew. She found all of it deeply disturbing. She was used to order and politeness. She'd expected a cordial welcome from a smiling academic who looked very much like Ivo, not an extremely hot man cursing a blue streak in Russian and waving around a phone.

"Fuck it. Jesus Fuck," he said, apparently in closing, since he pocketed his phone. He turned to her, shook his head and rubbed his eyes. "Okay. I'll drive you to Krasnodar, to the airport there, although I'm not sure we'll find you a flight out tonight."

She gawked. "What are you talking about?"

"Your return trip." Anger and disappointment warred for a moment on his face. "I'm sorry, but you have to go home."

"Home?" Charlotte looked down at the bags by her feet. "I'm not going home. I came here to help you. You're Dr. Mayfair, aren't you?"

"Call me Will." He leaned down to pick up her suitcase and shoulder bag. "And you *are* going home, I'm afraid. Car's over there."

She yanked on the strap of her bag, arresting him mid-step. "There's no way in hell I'm getting back on a plane right now. Just—stop for a minute." She fought with him for her luggage, trying not to stare at the impressive musculature of his arm. "I thought you needed me. I thought you searched for months to find someone who knows this dialect you're studying."

He gave her a hard look. "We did, which is the only reason I can think that Ivo would bring you here. He told me your name was Charlie Rowe. I assumed you were a guy. But you're a...woman." His eyes slid over her, from her travel-worn hair to her sensible Born shoes.

"And this is problem because?" she asked, bristling.

He didn't answer until his gaze snapped back to her eyes. "It's just a problem. Trust me."

He took her bag back, picked up the larger of her suitcases, and started toward his weathered SUV. She had no choice but to pick up the other suitcase and follow him.

"Krasnodar's only a couple hours away," he said over his shoulder. "We'll be there before nightfall."

Charlotte gritted her teeth. Will Mayfair was about to become acquainted with the concept of a "steel magnolia," because this southern girl wasn't getting on any plane. "I don't know what a Krasnodar is," she said, "but I know I'm not flying home tonight, or tomorrow either. Do you know how much planning and schedule-rearranging I had to do to come here?"

"I'm sorry to hear that, because you're leaving as soon as I can book you a flight."

She caught up to him, glaring at his rigidly composed face. "Ivo misled me too, you know. He said you'd be happy to see me. He said you needed my help."

"I do need your help," he snapped, walking faster. "Unfortunately, this isn't a place you should be at the moment."

"Is this about the local tensions thing?"

"It's not a 'thing.' There are real, actual cultural and political tensions brewing in this region of the country. Therefore, I would rather you didn't stay. If you were a man…"

"What's the difference if I'm a man or a woman?"

He scowled at her sideways. "Don't be an ugly American. There are places it matters."

Charlotte charged ahead of him, wincing as her suitcase banged against her shin. "Right back at you. Don't be an ugly…British person. Whatever they're called. Or Australian or Scot or whatever your accent is."

"A British person is called a Briton," he said in an affronted tone. "And that's what I am, if it even matters to someone as American as you."

Her mouth fell open at the unwarranted vitriol in his tone. "What do you mean by that? 'Someone as American as me?'"

He threw down her bags near his car and turned to her, arms crossed over his chest. "I mean that you're unpleasant, ethnocentric, and likely to get yourself in a lot of trouble here."

"You've sure got me pegged for someone who's known me all of ten minutes," she shot back. "And I don't think you can point fingers in the 'unpleasant' department. I've never met anyone so rude."

"I'm rude, am I?"

"You're the rudest Briton I've ever known."

"How many Britons have you known?"

"I've known...a few. But that doesn't matter."

"No," he agreed, popping the trunk. "What matters is that you're not a man and you can't stay here."

She watched him sling her bags into the back of his boxy gray vehicle. Even angry at him, she couldn't help ogling his shoulders and the perfectly sculpted ass framed obscenely by his ripstop shorts. *Good God. Cargos were never sexy until now, even if the guy wearing them is a total jackass.*

She didn't want to go home. Not because Dr. William Mayfair was a hot hunk of a man, but because she'd built up so many hopes for adventure. This was supposed to be the change in her life, the excitement she hadn't had for years. Or ever.

"Get in," he said, nodding at the passenger side.

"No."

They faced off, an infuriated Briton and Charlotte Rowe, who just wanted what she'd come for.

"You have to go home," he insisted. She could tell he was trying to convince himself, that he was frustrated too.

"You don't want me to go."

"That doesn't matter. What I want doesn't matter. I can't guarantee your safety here."

"I can't guarantee my safety back in Savannah. I could get killed crossing the street, or falling down a flight of stairs in a parking garage." She looked around at the unpopulated fields and mountains surrounding them. "What could possibly happen here?"

He gave her a dire look. "A war, maybe."

"Here? In the middle of nowhere? I just landed on a runway that I think was made of dirt. How does war happen here?"

"Believe me, it does, and the nearest embassies are ten hours away in Georgia. Not your Georgia," he added with a touch of snark. "The Russian one. It's a risk, that's all I'm telling you."

"But you stay."

"It's different. I'm a—"

"Man. Yes, I get it. I'm a woman. I have been all my life and I manage just fine."

He looked pained. "You don't understand. There are cultural differences here."

"I think I'm intelligent enough to deal with cultural differences. Maybe I'm *unpleasant* and *ethnocentric*, but I have half a brain. Ivo said I'd be safe as long as I had my passport."

"Yes, and Ivo has proven himself completely trustworthy thus far," Will said, rolling his eyes.

She stood her ground. "Women live here, right? They live here in Adygea?"

He sighed and then nodded. "Yes, women live here."

"Lots of women. A whole population full."

"Yes."

"So it's possible to live here and be safe, man *or* woman."

He rubbed his forehead and chuckled under his breath. "And stubborn, too. Wonderful." He looked around and then back at her. "Fine. If you want to stay, then stay. But I'm warning you, it'll be me and you at the campsite. I won't stay in Aleronsk, especially not now."

"You're full of warnings."

"All of which you ignore. The cabin's not big, and we'll be living there together. If that's not okay with you, tell me now."

Was it okay with her?

Her mother's voice promptly answered, *Of course it's not okay, Charlotte! Look at the man!*

With a grimace, she chased her mother out of her head. This wasn't about sex, or Will Mayfair's hotness. He was an academic, not a dating prospect. She would extend him the friendly professionalism owed a research partner and everything would be fine.

"It's perfectly okay with me, as long as we don't have to share a bed." Good God, why had she added that? Now she was imagining herself in bed with him. She held up her hands, feeling a flush creep into her face. "I'm not going to argue about living arrangements at this point."

He finally smiled at her, a wide, charming smile that frightened her more than anything they'd talked about to this point. *This isn't a joke, Charlotte*, her mother had said. *I'm afraid you'll find that out as soon as you get there.* It was feeling less like a joke by the moment and more like an…adventure. "I'm glad I'm staying," she burst out like a total nerd. "I'm ready for some adventure."

"Adventure?" He raised an eyebrow. "Be careful what you wish for." He reached out and guided her back a little. Charlotte's mind blared, *He's touching you!* but it was only so he could shut the trunk.

He opened the passenger-side door for her, then walked around the front of the car and climbed into the driver seat. *Be careful what you wish for.* Had he meant the words to sound so sharp? He wrenched the car into gear and drove out of the lot onto a pitted road that seemed to head straight for the nearest mountain. She buckled her seat belt as the vehicle picked up speed, bumping and bouncing over cracked pavement. It was an improvement from the prop plane, but only barely.

"You'll like the campsite," he said. "The setting's very beautiful."

She forced a smile in response, even though she hated camping. She'd gone a few times as a scout, until a run in with a snake put her off camping for good. She had actually picked up the snake, mistaking it for a stick. Her troop leader had explained the snake was harmless, but Charlotte felt betrayed by the unpredictability of nature. She shuddered at the memory, a shudder that was misinterpreted by Will.

"You can roll up the window if you're cold. The mountain air can feel crisp if you're not used to it."

"I'm fine. I like the mountain air."

"You may feel tired and short of breath for a while, until you get used to the higher elevation."

The higher elevation was the least of her concerns at the moment, but she wouldn't let him know that. None of this was turning out the way she'd envisioned, but she tried to convince herself everything was okay. She had a passport. They were out in the country. Surely a war would start in the more populated areas, and come with some advance warning.

She refused to give up so soon on her adventure, especially if this blond Adonis of a linguist was going to figure into it.

Be careful what you wish for, he'd said. Unfortunately, Charlotte wasn't in a careful state of mind.

* * * * *

Will searched his conscience—yes, he had one—to analyze whether he'd warned her adequately. He believed he had. Hell, he'd laid it all out for her. If she wouldn't go, it wasn't his fault. The truth was, he needed her here, and he was glad she'd decided to stay even though it was going to cause a boatload of problems. It wasn't just her vulnerability as a woman in an isolated mining region; it was that she would end up driving him mad.

She already was. She was regrettably beautiful, with delicate features and long, thick golden-brown hair. Her hazel eyes were large, her lips full, and her body curvy in all the right places. Damn Ivo. He couldn't just send a woman. He had to send an attractive one, and a bloody ornery one too. Beautiful women were trouble, and this one was already pissed at him. She didn't smile or make small talk, just stared out the window with her arms wrapped tightly around her waist.

"Hanging in there?" he asked. "We're almost to the cabin now."

"Cool," was all she replied, in a voice that sounded, well...cool. Frigid actually. She probably expected him to make inappropriate advances at the first possible opportunity. And damn it, he probably would. If only it hadn't been so long since he'd gotten any. That complicated matters, but he could exercise self-control as well as any man. Sure, she was pretty. Sure, he was thinking non-stop about kissing her and bending her head back to lick and suck on her stubborn little neck. Of course he was fantasizing about seducing her the moment they got to the cabin, but that's all it was. Fantasy.

Vivid fantasy, but still.

Will pulled into the camp clearing and drifted to a stop beside the sturdy cabin set down in the hillside. Across the clearing, the sun glinted off a small lake. They got out of the car and she seemed to unwind a little, drawing a deep breath and turning to take in the view. The Caucasus Mountains rose in a picturesque range that seemed endless, disappearing into scattered clouds in the distance. Charlotte gazed around at the panorama, her eyes wide.

"Wow. This is nothing like Savannah."

In that moment, in her breathless admiration, he wanted her even more than he'd wanted her before. "What's Savannah like?" he asked to distract himself from his lurid thoughts.

"Let's see. Buildings. Some parks and flowers. No mountains for sure. Savannah is low country. It's right next to the ocean."

"The nearest ocean here is the Black Sea, but that's a little far for a day trip. There are a lot of rivers and lakes, though."

She wandered closer to the shimmering body of water. "Do you fish there?"

"I swim there." *Naked.*

She sighed, staring into the distance. "The lake, the mountains. All that forest. Wow. Just wow. This is a whole new world."

He studied her a moment. "You like that, or not?"

"I like it."

"Why are you whispering?"

"It's so quiet here. Where are all the other people?"

"What other people?"

"You said this was a campground."

"A campsite. Not a campground."

He grabbed her bags out of the car and she followed him into the small structure he'd called home for over a year. The cabin was low and square, a utilitarian shelter that once housed overseers from the mines. It wasn't pretty but it was weather tight, which was a good thing. Will had grown used to rough lodgings over years of traveling to remote locales for his work, but Charlotte didn't strike him as the remote-locale type. Or particularly low maintenance.

They passed through the low-ceilinged main room that served as kitchen, dining room, and sitting room. He maneuvered around the rectangular table in the center, thinking he ought to have straightened up the papers scattered over the rough oak surface. She eyed the mess with a frown and then turned her gaze to the bare wood walls. Along the back wall were three doors—room, shared bathroom, and another room. He went through the door on the left and put down her suitcases.

"Sorry we're so cramped here."

He stepped back so she could look in. He felt self-conscious, like the place wasn't up to snuff, even though he'd never thought about it before now. Gah, five minutes in the house and she was already unhinging him. There was nothing wrong with the room. There was a lamp and a small end table, and a real bed, thanks to a particularly good budget year from the MacArthur people a few seasons back. There was a small armoire with drawers since there was no closet.

"It's better than sleeping in a tent," he said with a shrug.

Charlotte looked dubious. "Where do you stay?"

I'll stay here if you ask me to, Gorgeous. The words were on the tip of his tongue. He swallowed them with effort. "My room's on other side of the bathroom. It's not unusual in the field to have to share close quarters." He reached behind her to flip the deadbolt on the door. "There's a lock, in case you worry I'm a mad rapist."

She looked embarrassed. "I don't think you're a rapist."

"I must be losing my touch." He looked askance at her, raising one eyebrow. "Serial killer?"

She shook her head.

"Any type of criminal at all?"

"A petty fraudster, maybe," she said with a perfectly timed sniff. Will laughed out loud. If she was going to have a sense of humor under all that cool posturing, it would really throw a wrench in his efforts to resist her. He caught himself looking at her a few seconds too long. Such beautiful eyes.

Her smile faded and she hugged herself again. The self-protective gesture made him want to blurt out reassurances. Would that fix things or make them worse? *You'll be okay here. Everything will be okay. Forget everything I said.*

Jesus, he had to pull himself together. "Sorry it's not more posh," he said, scratching his forehead.

"It's fine."

"Not what you're used to."

"Not really, but that's okay."

"It's a pretty good house." He darted a look up toward the ceiling. "There might be a few spiders."

"A few?"

"Tons, actually. But not poisonous. Sort of big though. Well, really big. Hairy."

She scrutinized his face. "Please tell me you're joking."

He knew she wanted reassurance. Needed reassurance. He should have reassured her, but what he did instead was reach behind her again, this time to run a whisper-light touch up the back of her arm. She shrieked at the contact, leaping away from the door and brushing frantically at the imagined creature. Her reproachful glare was priceless.

"You completely suck," she said.

"Guilty," Will agreed. "Would you like something to eat?"

Chapter Three:
Lens

Charlotte had no idea how Will did it, but less than half an hour later, they were eating a meal of chicken with pasta and salad, and sharing a bottle of wine with a label in some language she couldn't read. She didn't care. It tasted so good, or perhaps she was just really hungry. While he'd prepared dinner, she'd unpacked her clothes and books and felt slightly more settled. The room wasn't bad. She tried to think of it as cozy rather than cramped. The bathroom had more or less modern fixtures, although it had probably been last updated in the fifties.

The main room was pleasantly uncluttered aside from the table, which Will had insisted on clearing himself. She'd never seen so many scraps of paper and notes scribbled everywhere. He seemed intense about his work. She just wasn't one hundred percent clear yet what that was. She put her wineglass down near the end of the meal and dug for more information.

"Ivo told me you were a linguist. What does that mean, exactly? I mean, what do you do?"

Will leaned back, stretching his arms over his head. He probably hadn't meant it as an act of seduction, but Charlotte's mouth went dry and she had to reach for her wine again.

"Linguistics is a general name for what I do," he explained. "I'm sort of an anthropologist of languages. North Caucasus languages."

"Why North Caucasus languages? Is your family from this area?"

"Not at all. Russian was the language in vogue when I started university. I wanted to be different so I studied Circassian, Adyghe, Kabardian, Chechen."

"Have you always been interested in languages?"

"Forever. I started collecting language dictionaries when I was five."

"How many do you speak?"

He considered for a moment, mentally counting in his head. "I don't speak them all, so much as compare them. But I know eleven or twelve pretty fluently, not including related dialects. Maybe...in all, dialects included...thirty or so?"

He couldn't have been much older than her, and he spoke all those languages? "You're a savant."

"No, nothing like that. Anyway, I don't know everything I need to know. The dialect in that document—I can't puzzle it out." He said *can't* like *cawn't*. "Believe me, I've tried to put some lingual system together, but..." He waved his hand, a shadow of frustration falling over his face.

Charlotte frowned. "It's Adyghe."

"It's not Adyghe. I know Adyghe."

"My grandfather told me it was Adyghe when he spoke it to me."

"I mean, it's some derivation of Adyghe, but it's an old dialect, one your family probably took away as emigrants. No one around here knew it. We had scores of people out." He leaned forward and gave her an assessing look. "If no one else in your family still speaks it, it's possible you're a 'lens.'"

There was something unsettling in the way he looked at her. "What's a lens?"

"It's an acronym for Last Native Speaker." He shifted and shrugged, breaking the strange tension. "All languages die eventually. A frustrating problem for people like me."

"Maybe I am a lens. Is it anything like being an oracle?"

Will chuckled and rose to clear the table. "I don't know. I guess we'll see tomorrow when you have a go at the text."

Charlotte got up to help, carrying stoneware and utensils as dated and durable as everything else in the cabin. For the first time, a horrible thought occurred to her. "What if I take a look at this book and can't figure out any of it? What if I only knew the part Ivo showed me, and the rest is nonsense?"

If her words alarmed him, he didn't show it. "If you can't make it out, I suppose I'll have to take you around back and shoot you," he said lightly.

Charlotte laughed. "From lens to corpse. That sounds about right."

Their eyes met with such warmth that Charlotte took a step back. He was way too charming, and for sure too good-looking. She needed some distance. They both turned their attention to the dishes. He washed, she dried. They stacked them right on the counter because there were no cabinets. There wasn't much of anything. No Internet, no cable. The electricity came from a generator and the water came from a well. After dinner, they took the rest of the wine out to the front porch and rocked in rickety chairs crafted from bent branches. Charlotte eyed hers with suspicion, but found it surprisingly comfortable to rock in. The seat was worn smooth. "Did you and Ivo make these chairs?"

"Yes. On one of our bored Saturdays. We also used sand from the bottom of the lake to cook up these wine glasses." He held his glass up to catch the light of the setting sun and scrutinized it with a comically serious air. Charlotte started giggling. Damn wine. Charlotte Rowe *never* giggled. She set her glass on the porch rail and ran a hand over the arm of the chair.

"I guess in a place like this, you have to find ways to stay busy."

As soon as she said it, it sounded suggestive to her. A corner of Will's mouth quirked up, but he only took another sip of wine and asked, "So what do you do in Savannah to stay busy, Charlotte?"

Charlotte. The way he pronounced her name, with his lazy English accent... "I'm an organizer," she said, clearing her throat. "I organize people's homes."

He looked surprised. "You do that for a living?"

"Yes, I have my own business. It's called OrganizeNation. You know, like 'organization' but with the extra 'n' in the middle."

"OrganizeNation. I like it. Clever, with a touch of megalomania to make it interesting. And business is good?"

Charlotte nodded. "You'd be surprised how hard it is for people to keep themselves organized. How grateful they are when you show them how."

"So you teach them what to do? How to sort out their houses?"

"We do the initial organization, closets and cabinets and stuff, but hopefully they keep things up after we go."

"How much are you paid for this important work?'"

Charlotte didn't know him well enough to tell if he was being sarcastic. "I'm making a very good living at it," she said, "and I like what I do."

His eyes never left her. She felt pinned, like he was analyzing her. Dissecting her like some dialect. "So what's your favorite thing about your job?" he persisted. "Mucking out the clutter? Making sense of people's chaos?" Again, that wide, enthralling smile. "I rather enjoy chaos myself, when I'm in the mood for it."

Charlotte's mind immediately conjured lascivious thoughts about chaos and Will being in the mood. She pulled at her ear and sat up straighter. "Honestly, I prefer serenity to chaos."

"Ah, serenity. Now that I know it's important to you, I'll work on my organization. It's never been my strong suit."

She laughed. "Languages have never been mine. I mean, I liked speaking Adyghe with my grandfather, but I didn't go around learning a zillion other dialects like you." She looked at him sideways. God, now she was flirting with him. Embarrassingly, he chose not to flirt back. He looked at her like someone might look at a particularly charming niece.

"You're probably so good at organizing because you like to help people. Otherwise you wouldn't have come all this way to translate for someone you don't even know."

"Well, Ivo begged me."

"I imagine he did. He's desperate to know what's in that book, and I'd like to catalog the language while I have the chance. Before it dies out."

She stared out at the mountains in the waning light. "Before I die, you mean?"

"Yes."

They both fell silent. After a while, she asked, "Do you really think no one else on earth knows that language? Just me?"

"Trust me, we looked. If someone else does, they're like you. Hiding somewhere far off."

"I wasn't hiding."

"Well, what were you doing?" he asked with that expression she couldn't quite interpret yet.

Charlotte thought a moment. "Waiting, I guess."

* * * * *

Will didn't want to go to bed. He could have sat on the porch another four hours drinking wine and talking with her, but she was tired. Her eyes were closing, her lilting voice growing softer.

"You should turn in." He aimed for a brisk, impersonal tone. "I'd like to start on the document tomorrow, if it's not too soon."

"Not at all. I'm ready to get started." She stood and stretched with a lovely spreading smile. God, she might be a little drunk. Caucasus wines were excellent but potent. He had to look away from her before he said something stupid. Maybe he was a little drunk too.

"I'll see you in the morning," he said. "Thanks again for coming all this way to help us. And I'm sorry about the scene at the airport. You took me by surprise, being a Charlotte and not a Charlie."

"You took me by surprise too." She didn't elaborate, but he thought he saw a hint of a blush steal across her cheeks. God help him, it would be so easy to romance her right here, right now; they were both of them half gone. They could blame everything on the wine in the morning.

"Well, good night," she said, with one last look around the site. There was nothing to see, only the dim outline of mountains and the faintest of light from Aleronsk. For months, since Ivo had gone, Will had stared at the dark night alone, not that it bothered him. He'd always been a loner, a geek. At some point he'd discovered that women found him attractive. That had been a shock, but a welcome shock. He was pretty sure Charlotte found him attractive, and just as sure she didn't intend to do anything about it.

Well, fuck. He supposed it was better that way. He thought about heading in and playing a few rounds of a shooter game on the ancient Nintendo, but he didn't want to keep her up. Honestly, Will missed Ivo. If the old man were here now, they would have talked—quietly of course—about the mysterious lens Charlotte Rowe. It wasn't unusual for obscure dialects to flourish in places far from their origin, while the language evolved back in the homeland until they were two separate tongues.

For Will, it was all part of the fun. Language was a mystery, a never-ending one, and he liked playing detective. He never tired of collecting language fragments and clues and analyzing them. He'd piece them together like a puzzle until a lingual system emerged that made sense. In the best cases, the completed puzzle revealed something about the people who spoke the language. Over the years, he'd come to look at words not just as communication tools, but as palpable pieces of people, like their hearts or their feet. Their noses. All people had words, every culture, and those who couldn't make words with their mouths found ways to make them with their hands. If hands didn't work, they used feet, or blinks of their eyes. When Will had nightmares, they were about becoming wordless, speechless. He would imagine himself paralyzed, head to toe, even his eyelids unable to blink, and wake up in a gasping sweat.

Heh. Linguist nightmares. And funny, considering many days went by when he spoke to no one at all. But now Charlotte was here, bringing her own unique dialect and tones, even though she was speaking the same language as him. She said things like *wayle* instead of *well*, *naht* instead of *not*. *Linz* instead of *lens*. She lingered over syllables he bit off, and exaggerated her vowels to cosmic proportions. But he wasn't here to study her English.

You're not here to seduce her either.

He rubbed his forehead and sighed. It would happen eventually. It just would. They'd wear down and give in. What would she be like in bed? Very controlled, Will thought. Very controlling, maybe, with her organizing obsession. He wasn't one to put up with being controlled or managed. They'd butt heads, each grasping for the upper hand.

Bloody hell, that got him hot. Will had an instant, vivid image of trapping her wrists and drawing them over her head, holding them against the wall as he forced her to submit to his kiss. Then she'd pull away and slap him Scarlett O'Hara style, and he'd grab her and carry her to the bed while she pretended to struggle—

Perhaps that was actually some scene from *Gone with the Wind*. Anyway, he wanted to do that to her. They could act out the whole damn movie as long as they ended up in bed together. Once there, he would treat her to a very chaotic, unorganized fuck and she could deal with it. He'd have to remember to pick up some condoms next time he went into town on his own.

But first…first he would take her to Aleronsk's museum to look at the book. A complete mystery, and she would be his code breaker. At one time, there were probably thousands of people who spoke that dialect. Will imagined them all ranged around her, watching, waiting, their fingers crossed. Charlotte was it, the last chance for their words and culture to be preserved. He knew she didn't feel the weight of responsibility, didn't understand what a miracle she was. He'd explain it to her one day.

But for now they had to get moving, get the project started if they were going to see it through. He hoped local tensions ebbed, and the dangers he worried about never came to fruition. He barely knew Charlotte Rowe, but he liked her and he didn't want her to come to any harm. He liked her pluck. Hell, she'd persevere just fine on sheer stubbornness. The truth was, he already liked her way too much.

Chapter Four: Aleronsk

Charlotte woke the next morning still in her clothes, jetlagged and hung over, cursing wine of dubious origins. Maybe he'd drugged her, because she'd slept like a rock. *He didn't drug you, Charlotte. He's nice. In a dangerously charming way.*

She moaned as she sat up, then wondered if he was out in the other room listening to her. He would have that expression on his face, that cryptic, knowing smile. Good lord, she needed a shower and a good tooth brushing, and then she'd feel human again. She dragged her bag into the bathroom, dug out fresh clothes and a bath towel that smelled like home. She locked the latch on the door to Will's room, then crossed to the curtained, claw-footed bath tub and turned on the water. There was almost no water pressure. She looked for the shower toggle only to discover there wasn't one. No toggle. And no shower.

She shut the water off, crossed back to the door and flung it open. Will sat at the table, looking stubbly and morning-ish. But still hot, damn it.

"Where is the shower?"

He didn't even look up from his laptop. "What do you think this is, Club Med? And don't use too much water in your bath, please. There's a limited amount. I find it easier to bathe in the lake."

Charlotte gawked. "In the lake? That's disgusting."

He shrugged. "I do laundry there too. It's fresh water. It comes down off the mountains. It's probably cleaner than the water from your tap at home."

She shut the door before she could say what she thought of his fresh, dirty mountain laundry water. Had he noticed she had a lot of hair? She was supposed to wash it in a bath tub? Or worse, a lake, with God knew what kind of toxic mountain amoebas floating around, along with his dirty laundry germs? She eyed the porcelain fixture warily and took a deep breath. *Don't fall apart over this. Don't be a total neurotic female like he expects you to be.*

She went back to the door to the main room and locked it. She didn't want him walking in on her. It was going to take forever to wash the tub, and then wash her hair—

"You don't have to lock it. I won't come barging in."

She opened the door and glared at him. "I'm not locking you out."

"I'm the only other person here. You're locking me out."

"I'm more worried about the spiders."

"Spiders can't open doors. Now, the bears..."

Charlotte rolled her eyes and closed the door. From the other side she heard a clipped "Good morning to you too!"

She ignored it, locking the door again and giving the tub a thorough going over with cleaning solution she found under the sink. At least she hoped it was cleaning solution, since she couldn't read the foreign text on the side of the bottle. By the time she finished wrestling with her hair and bathing, it seemed like a full hour had gone by, and her stomach was growling. She dressed in jeans and a tee and went out to the main room to find Will gone. His room was empty too, the door ajar. She pushed down a frisson of panic. Where was he? If something happened to him— *a bear!*—she had no idea where the nearest town was or how to speak the local language. She didn't even know how to drive the manual transmission in his ancient SUV. *Oh my God.*

She forced herself to calm down and poured a cup of coffee in the kitchen. The car was still there, so he hadn't gone far. The windows were open, admitting cool morning breezes. She made some toast and took it over by the window to look out.

What she saw nearly made her drop it on the floor. Will Mayfair, language savant extraordinaire, was climbing out of the lake naked as hellfire. The impulse to shield her eyes was overcome by plain curiosity. *Well, at least you know where he is now.* Yes, he was very hard to miss. He shook out his light tousled hair, styling it with a careless brush of fingers before he reached for a towel draped over a nearby bush. She expected him to wrap it around himself...to...to cover himself, for God's sake. Not that he had anything to be ashamed of. At all.

Oh geez, Charlotte. Stop staring. He toweled off like some careless god in the sunshine. Even from across the clearing, she could appreciate the strength of his body, the crisp masculinity of his movements. A turn of his head, the lift of his arm. The way he bent down to towel off his legs. And God...his...*Jesus.* Even that, she could see from her vantage point, which meant he could also probably see her if he turned this way.

As if on cue, he looked over at the cabin, at the very window where she stood gaping at him. She leaped back and ducked at the same time, then ran to sit at the table. She pretended to be extremely interested in her coffee when she heard him enter. He walked into his room and closed the door without so much as a word to her. Just as well. She couldn't have spoken anyway.

She finished her toast and locked herself in her bedroom to dry her hair—another exercise in frustration. Of course her American hairdryer didn't work with the cabin's electrical outlets. She might as well throw the thing away. She was about to do that when a small movement caught her eye. She looked at the ceiling over the door, not believing. She screwed her eyes shut and crawled onto her bed, as if that might offer her some protection.

Please, please be gone next time I look.

She nearly jumped out of her skin when Will knocked on her door. "Charlotte, are you ready? Let's go into Aleronsk. The museum opens at nine."

"I can't come out," she yelled.

"Why not?"

"Because there's a spider the size of my head over the door."

He rattled the doorknob. "I'd love to come in and help you, but you locked me out again. Throw something at it. It'll run off."

"Throw something at it? It would probably laugh at me."

She could have sworn she heard a chuckle. Damn him. She looked around for something to sacrifice to the cause. In the end she threw the useless hairdryer and missed by a mile. The spider scuttled up into a corner of the high ceiling and disappeared, spooked by the flying plastic object, or perhaps by her ear-splitting screams.

* * * * *

He'd originally thought she wouldn't come to Aleronsk with him because of his stunt at the lake. Well, it wasn't a stunt. What was he supposed to do, bathe in his clothes? She was the one who'd stood at the window spying on him. He hadn't been completely sure of it until he'd come in and seen how red she'd blushed. She'd blushed again when he held open the door of the car for her. He wondered if she had any idea how often she blushed, or how much it gave away. He was pretty sure he could have her begging for sex with him in a day or two, if he put his mind to it.

But then, he didn't know what a serenity lover like her would make of a horny pervert like him. He didn't generally like things too tame between the sheets, and she seemed as prim as a puritan. He shouldn't get too revved up about what would probably amount to mild, guilt-ridden sex while she protested the whole time about how she shouldn't be doing it. Reality—better than a cold shower. Or a cold dip in the lake.

He glanced over at his silent passenger. One of her legs jittered up and down.

"Still buggered about the spider, love?"

She turned to him. "What does that mean, buggered?"

He started to answer and thought better of it. "Never mind."

"And why did you call me love?"

"Because you're so lovely." She snorted and turned away. "It's a thing English people say. Let me think if I can ask my question in American English." He cleared his throat and tried again. "Are you still bothered about that spider, dude?" He used the broadest fake American accent he could muster, and was rewarded with a gem of a laugh. Better, her leg stopped jumping for a moment.

"No, I'm not still bothered about the spider. Or buggered about it or anything. I'm just anxious about...you know."

"If you can't read it, you can't read it. Life goes on."

"But you'll be disappointed."

He looked over at her as they turned onto Aleronsk's main street. "You don't owe me anything. All you'll get if you're successful will be a share of whatever books or articles we publish, and that won't amount to much. I'm still shocked you agreed to come at all."

"I told you why I came here. I needed a change."

"That's right. Adventure, you said. Well, look around. The adventure's beginning."

The town was small, but busy with people. He saw all the usual suspects. Mostly men, a few women of questionable character. Older women who owned shops to make a living. There were very few older men to be found around Aleronsk. Mining was a hard way of life. He doubted she would put all that together in a few minutes, or even during the short duration of her time here. She stared at a cluster of miners on the corner as he turned down the side street that housed the region's antiquities museum.

"They're so dirty," she said.

"Mining is dirty work. I stick out here like a sore thumb. Too clean."

"You could stop swimming in the lake. Especially naked."

He laughed. "So that's what's got you buggered. You know, if you wanted to check out what I have to offer, you only had to ask."

She held out a hand, cutting him off. "I was not checking you out. I was looking out the window when you revealed yourself to me. That's illegal where I come from, by the way. Indecent exposure."

"Perfectly legal here." His glib comment went ignored as she turned her attention to the ramshackle building where he pulled up and parked.

"This is a museum?" she asked.

"The outside is unassuming, but that's par for the course around here. There's a lot of brilliant stuff inside."

As they climbed out of the car, a few miners stopped and turned to take her in. She gazed back, as bold and curious as she pleased. It both impressed and horrified him. He came up behind her and guided her away.

"Don't look at them like that."

"Like what?"

"Just don't look at them. It doesn't translate culturally, okay?"

"What does that mean?"

"They see it as an invitation. Around here, women in the streets don't look at men directly unless they're...selling something."

"Oh."

"Yeah. Keep away from them. They're not the Southern gentlemen you're used to. A lot of them are soldiers."

He threw one last look at the retreating men, trying to communicate what she wasn't—that she was off limits. She had already turned her attention to the small lobby of displayed antiquities in Aleronsk's museum. There were ornate vases and shabby shards of pottery, all proudly labeled and displayed.

"What are they digging for?" she asked, looking over her shoulder.

"What?"

"Those miners. What are they mining?"

"Gold. Silver. Other things."

"Gold? Really?"

"Why do you think this isolated mountainous wasteland is so hotly competed for? There's oil here too, and the Russians want it."

"I thought these were Russians."

Will cringed, hoping the stern faced man at the desk didn't understand what Charlotte had just said. "They are and they aren't," he whispered next to her ear. "It's a long story." A long story he'd tell her later. For now, he turned his most disarming smile on the museum clerk and presented his authorization papers from the Adyghe Office of Antiquities. After the man scrutinized them closely, he led them to a small back room with a desk against the wall, and several locked cases. He went to a case in the corner and produced a smaller box that looked fairly new. He unlocked it with a key and opened the top, placing the box and its contents on the desk.

Then, with a look down his nose at Charlotte, the clerk left.

"Come on," said Will. He felt a little breathless. The language that had eluded him was within his grasp, right there on the desk. With Charlotte's help, he could resurrect the lost dialect, and Ivo could finally know what was written on the pages. He set up his laptop on one side of the desk. Charlotte started to sit on the opposite side and he stopped her.

"No. Right here." It came out an order, rather rude. She complied anyway, taking the seat beside him. She reached out to touch the cover of the decaying volume. "Stop!"

She pulled her hand back as if she'd been burned. Instead of an apology, he offered her a pair of white cotton gloves.

"I didn't know," she said, pursing her lips.

"It's okay. It's rather fragile. Let me do the handling and page turning."

"Fine. So what do you want me to do? You want me to read and tell you what it says?"

"Yes. Sort of. I want you to tell me the words in the dialect first, phonetically. I'll record that. It's called transcription. Then tonight we'll go back over the text and you can tell me the nearest English equivalent of what the words mean. That's called translation."

She looked at the thick volume, raising her eyebrows. The question was obvious enough.

"It's two hundred and eighty-eight pages long. It will be a lot of work. But what else have we got to do?" he asked with a smile. He could think of a few things, but nothing to mention at the moment, not in the cramped musty room with the frowning clerk hovering. Charlotte took a deep breath and in that moment she seemed almost painfully beautiful to him. A wonder. A lens. Resurrector of lost words.

"Charlotte," he said, just before she read out the first words. She stopped, surprised, looking over at him. The desk was so small, they were shoulder to shoulder. Their knees touched. He thought perhaps he ought to say *thank you* again, or maybe even, *I love you*. At that moment, he loved her passionately. She was oblivious to him though, turning back to the book before her.

"This looks so old. Someone many, many years ago—"

"Hundreds of years ago."

"Hundreds of years ago wrote these words by hand. His pen brushed across this very page." She looked up at him. "It would have been a man, yes?"

"Yes, I think so."

Her fingers hovered over the yellowed parchment as if she tried to absorb the aura of the book, draw from it some long-ago whispers of meaning or feeling. Will imagined the writer of the text bent over the pages just as she was now, thinking about what to write. What if some wrinkle in the universe was to unite the two, the original author, and his newest—and probably last—reader, Charlotte Rowe of Savannah, Georgia? What would the man make of her? It was as if Charlotte's hand covered over the hand of that ancient writer, helping his words find voice after centuries of silence. The man would have liked her, Will thought. He would have marveled at her red lips and dark gold hair, and the smattering of freckles on her nose. She would have smiled at the writer, and the man couldn't have resisted her charm. Will wanted to smile, or maybe he wanted to weep over it all.

Instead he stayed silent and let her read.

They spent an hour or more on the first paragraph. Together they settled on the phonetic pronunciation of vowels and consonants, and added the letters the present-day Adyghe language lacked. He learned to work in and around her accent, adjusting phonemes as they went. Hearing the foreign tongue from her lips, the language clicked and opened to him. It brought a fierce rush of excitement. All his senses were heightened, his aural faculties at full attention. He watched Charlotte's lips obsessively, listened hard so he didn't miss a single sound. He asked her to repeat, and repeat again. She did, never showing frustration or impatience. She read, read, re-read, as many times as he asked.

He could have gone on for days charting each phoneme and word as it came. Already the constructions were starting to make sense in his head and he didn't want to stop, but the clerk sent them home at quarter to five. A request to take the book and return with it in the morning was met with laughter. It wasn't until they got out to the car and started back that his strange heightened state began to dissipate.

There was still the translation to come, which was Ivo's interest more than his. She had given him quick, offhand translations as they worked through the first few pages. Gods and goddesses, hills and mountains, a heroic people. Local mythology, which Ivo had guessed.

Will wanted to lay her down and make love to her for hours.

He knew it was just the work. The thrill. The excitement of finally cracking a dialect that had stumped him. Not to mention the fact that it had been him and his tireless palm for the last half year, since he'd been home and convinced a friend-with-benefits to benefit him.

"You're quiet," she said.

He glanced over at her, thankful they were in the SUV and not at the cabin. "I'm thinking about what to make for dinner," he lied.

"You should let me make dinner tonight."

"Can you cook?" She bit her lip. She looked adorable. "I'll take that as a no. Don't worry. You keep the cabin serene and organized, and I'll cook. I have a pretty good system worked out. I was thinking about stopping for fresh bread to eat tonight with soup. Easy."

"Easy is good."

"Are you very tired?" *Don't! You shouldn't sleep with her!*

"No. Not really. Just relieved that I can read that book you're so hyped about. And looking forward to eating well tonight."

"I'll be sure to eat you well every night." *Oh, man.* "I mean, I'll make sure you eat well every night. Yeah."

She laughed softly, but he clamped his mouth shut. He wasn't saying one more word to her in his current state of mind.

* * * * *

After dinner they set up at the table the same way they'd set up in the back room of the museum. It was hard for Charlotte to concentrate, sitting so close to him. He smelled like soap and mountain air and sunshine. When he smiled at her, it felt like standing in the sun.

He printed out the transcribed text with space between each line, and she translated the words below so he could enter them into his laptop. It was slow going at first. She felt the weight of the language on her shoulders. If she got it wrong, there was no one else to get it right.

"Just do your best," he said when she questioned him for the tenth time. "Make your best guess at what the writer meant."

"What if it doesn't translate exactly?"

"Use the word you think comes closest."

Charlotte focused on the story, biting the tip of her pen and trying to imagine what the writer's voice might have sounded like. Not his actual voice, but how he would have written in English. The tone of the piece was clear enough from the start. Grandiose and important. Mythology, Will had said. She paused again, chewing harder on the tip of her pen.

"Hungry?" he asked.

"What?"

"You're consuming your pen."

She lowered it. "Sorry. Nervous habit."

He returned to pecking out her notes. Fifteen minutes or so passed in silence, broken only by her pen tapping on the tabletop. He stopped her twice, telling her it made it difficult for him to concentrate. The third time he pushed his chair back with a *scrittcch*, stood and stretched. Charlotte couldn't help noticing a flat expanse of stomach and golden blond hair that probably trailed all the way down to... *God, don't think about it.*

"You want some coffee?"

Charlotte cleared her throat, hoping she wasn't blushing. "Coffee?"

"Yeah, you know, it's a dark type liquid thing? You drink it hot? Brewed from coffee beans?"

She was starting to hate his sarcastic side. "I know what coffee is. And yes, I would like some," she added in a softer tone. "With sugar, please."

She watched him rattle around the tiny kitchen, brewing a pot of coffee. Even this he did in a peculiarly masculine and rugged way, grinding the beans in a noisy contraption and splashing the water into the machine as if the niceties of exact measurement were below him. Lord, he was sexy. When had she turned so man-crazy? Her last couple boyfriends had been such braying, unfaithful asses she'd sworn off men altogether. Her mother would have been overjoyed to find Charlotte developing a renewed interest, except that Adele Rowe wouldn't approve of Will Mayfair. He wasn't wealthy, or possessed of high-placed connections, unless you counted the MacArthur folks. He could be sarcastic, abrupt and straightforward. Adele would call him mannerless. *But what do* you *think of him, Charlotte?*

He returned with a delicate porcelain sugar bowl, so out of place on the scarred tabletop.

"Sweets for the sweet."

She laughed politely and he returned again with two mugs of coffee. He drank his black, watching with a look of distaste as she shoveled three spoonfuls of sugar into her cup.

"You are, aren't you?" he asked. "Sweet?"

"I guess," said Charlotte.

"'I guess,'" he mimicked, doing a dead on impression of her gentle southern lilt. "You put so much sugar in there, I can't believe it tastes right."

Was he trying to be charming or churlish? "Yes, Dr. Mayfair, I put lots of sugar in my coffee. Sorry I'm not a cool black-coffee-drinking Brit like you."

"Oh, I'm cool?" He chuckled. "This from the ice queen."

Churlish then. He looked back at his notes, and she felt dismissed as abruptly as she'd felt attacked. If this was how British people flirted, she found it a little off-putting. She picked up her pen, trying to focus on the text rather than the way he addled her. She tried to concentrate on shades of meaning, but all she could think of was the knee brushing against hers and the hand on the table beside her, lightly freckled on the back, with a dusting of white-gold hair. He leaned closer, pointing to a section of her notes.

"For this, do you mean leap? Like, jump across?"

"*Me' ba' zhe*. Jump. Leap. Either one. To jump across a mountain. Leap might be better, come to think of it. But then leap sounds so...I don't know."

"Frou-frou?"

She nodded. "Better go with jump." She had barely returned to her notes when she heard his voice again over the typing on his keyboard.

"Do you have a boyfriend?"

"What?"

He stopped typing and looked at her, enunciating each word with exaggerated clarity. "Do you have a boyfriend?"

"I heard you the first time. I just don't know why you're asking me."

"I'm curious."

She turned it back on him, with his smug smile and his swanky black coffee. "Do you have a girlfriend?"

"Do you see a girlfriend?" he asked, looking around.

"I mean back in England."

"No, I don't."

"Wife?"

"No."

"Ex-wife?"

He laughed. "No."

"Kids?"

"God, no. I'm not family-man material."

She tapped her pen on the table, vaguely annoyed by this revelation even though it didn't matter to her. He glared at her hand.

"Could you stop that? It's driving me insane." He rubbed his eyes and thrust her notes across to her again. "This word. It means once? Or one?"

She looked at the word he pointed to. "*Zhey*. Yeah, once. At one time. Then."

"Which is it?"

"I don't know, it's not exact. It's like...at that time."

"Once upon a time?"

"Yeah, once upon a time," she drawled. "Why don't you write that?"

"These aren't fairy tales, princess."

She rolled her eyes and almost started tapping on the table again before his tsk arrested her. She put the pen down and met him eye to eye.

"Why are you so keyed up tonight? I thought you'd be happy that we've started."

"I am happy." He looked back at his screen, raising his eyebrows as if she were the oversensitive one. "I was only curious if you had a boyfriend, Princess Charlotte."

"Yes, if you must know, I have about twenty of them. And don't call me princess."

"Why not?"

"Because you're not my prince."

He stood abruptly, closing his laptop and carrying his coffee mug to the kitchen. "I'm going into town for a bit. You better stay here."

She stared down into the light sugary brown of her coffee until he'd gathered his car keys and slammed the door. What the hell had gotten into him? Where did he get off, prying into her personal life in that mocking manner of his? But she'd grilled him with personal questions too, and he'd answered her clearly: *Not family-man material.* In other words, not relationship material, so she needed to get over her crush on him, and fast. She needed to stop thinking about Will Mayfair altogether. He wasn't the reason she was here—the dialect was.

It would help if she could get out of the cramped cabin for a while. There were still a couple hours before sunset, enough time to go for a walk. She wasn't going anywhere near the lake though, because it would remind her of him that morning, rising out of the water all naked and muscular and...naked...

God, pull it together, Charlotte.

What she needed was a peaceful, meditative walk to get her shit together, because she'd had enough of heartbreak and failed relationships, and because what she felt for Will Mayfair wasn't organized or sensible at all.

Chapter Five: A Walk

Will drove the car full out. He skidded the curves and took the potholes. The whine of the engine did nothing to drown out the sounds in his mind, novel, guttural phonemes tinged with a shadow of graceful southern American accent. *Charlottelanguage.* It was driving him out of his mind.

He was able to separate the true language from her accent, even through the noise of his frustrated longing. He knew enough of related dialects and her own lilting speech to do it easily. The inflections and consonants of Charlotte's English could comprise a study all their own. Maybe he'd do that study someday. In fact, he'd like to do a study of Charlotte's exclamations in the throes of passion. Now that would interest him, although he doubted the MacArthur fellows would approve the grant.

With a sigh he turned and headed toward Aleronsk's general store and pharmacy. The sign out front was obscured with glare from the piercing rays of the early-evening sun. Everything was heightened at this time of day. The light, the crowds of men. The risk. Thank God she hadn't argued about being left back at the cabin. Not just because all the miners were heading into town after shift to drink, but because he was going to buy some goddamned condoms and he didn't want her to know.

He went into the shop and wandered around a few minutes, lollygagging. He picked out some chocolate bars. Didn't all women love chocolate? The chocolate here was awful but he'd need an excuse when he went back, to explain why he'd bolted off so quickly. Great, pretending to be ruled by chocolate cravings. Very masculine. He'd sunk this low.

He couldn't get it out of his head, the sight of her bent over her notebook, concentrating, working so hard to help him. She was a natural at translation, perfect in pitch. *So great were the gods, so great were the goddesses, so replete in size and stature, that the mountains were only hills to them, mere knolls. The dark sea was as a trickling creek, easy to jump over.* And an organizer-for-hire from Savannah could fly ten thousand kilometers and singlehandedly bring a dead language back to life.

He blew out his breath, went to stand in front of the condom display. He scanned the colored boxes, feeling unaccountably edgy. He'd poked at her, asked if she had a boyfriend, and why? If she had, would it have stopped him trying to seduce her? Not a bloody chance. Any boyfriend she had was too far away to concern Will, and she didn't have one, anyway. Why couldn't he just topple her into bed and not feel fucking guilt about it? She wanted him—the signals were obvious—and God knew he wanted her.

Why tiptoe around each other when the truth was so clear?

He paid for his condoms and chocolate and returned to the car, squinting up at the sun as it dropped behind the trees. Soon enough the sun would make an appearance in the mythology text. Suns always did. No culture ignored the glowing ball in the sky, the circle of fire that sustained life and yet pinned man beneath its glaring scrutiny. In the light of the sun, nothing could be hidden. Nothing *should* be hidden. It occurred to Will he ought to just tell Charlotte how he felt, how attracted he was to her. Confess that he thought about molesting her hourly, and toss the fuckbuddy invitation into her court.

With a new sense of purpose, he bumped over the pitted path back to camp and pulled into the clearing. If she responded the way he hoped to his newfound candor, he'd be ready to go with contraceptives—and chocolate for afterward. He was truly the man. He didn't let himself think about problems like the incompatibility of their natures, or the caliber of quality control in Russian condom factories.

He strode to the cabin feeling like a weight had been lifted off his shoulders. Honesty, what a novel prospect. Not that he was generally dishonest. He'd found over the years that, for whatever reason, women didn't make a lot of emotional demands on him. Or perhaps it was he who subconsciously avoided getting emotionally involved. But he was emotionally involved now, for better or worse, because he'd found a lens and she was beautiful.

"Charlotte!" As soon as he stepped inside he yelled her name, lest he lose his resolve. "Charlotte? I have chocolate."

She was nowhere in the main room, not in the kitchen or dining area or the sitting area in the corner. "Charlotte?"

No answer. Surely she wasn't sleeping already? It was only just growing dark. He drifted over to her door. It was slightly ajar. He knocked, and when there was no answer he pushed it open. Empty. He checked the bathroom and found it empty too. When he checked his own room, his heart started to race. He ran outside.

"Charlotte! Answer me. If you're hiding, this isn't funny."

He did two frantic searches of the perimeter before he faced the fact that she wasn't there. That she'd gone somewhere without him. He looked around, his mind turning in a furious whirl. He hadn't seen her on the road home. Unless she'd plunged into the dense woods and started down the side of the mountain, the only other direction she could have gone was down the path that led to the miner's ghetto.

The idea of it had him sprinting for the car.

* * * * *

God, it felt great to get some space. The smell was different here...piney, like evergreens and woods. Charlotte missed the flower smell of her neighborhood in Savannah, with its artfully landscaped squares. Still, the weather was perfect and this tiny corner of the world had its own charms.

Her trip had been a pretty cool experience so far, except for the spiders. And the lack of showering facilities. Thinking about showering facilities got her thinking about the lake, and a certain devastatingly handsome Englishman. She put that thought out of her mind and refocused herself on enjoying the scenery. The exercise and fresh air would be good for her lingering jet lag, and the realization that she wasn't one hundred percent reliant on him was bracing too. The path was already widening into a near approximation of a road, which meant she was unlikely to end up lost in some forest.

She looked up at the sky, checking the light. She remembered his warnings about the town after dark, but it wasn't even dusk, and she wouldn't make it to town anyway. These were quiet streets with rows of cabins similar to theirs—a campground after all. The small front yards and porches were deserted. An American hip-hop song blasted from somewhere, and she was so delighted by the sound of home she almost started singing along. She felt so isolated in the cabin with Will; hearing the music reassured her she was still in the twenty-first century. There were people here like everywhere else. It was a comforting thought.

A little farther down, she heard the strains of some news or radio program. She wondered why Will lived out in the woods when this place was so much closer and obviously wired with at least basic cable services. He'd told her the nearest reliable Internet access was in Maykop, but the people here were picking up some kind of TV or radio signals at least.

She slowed, looking up at the sky again. The sun, which had been so glaringly bright ten minutes ago, was disappearing behind the mountains. She'd better get back. She wasn't sure if Will had been joking about the bears, but she didn't want to come across one in the darkness. She turned and started back the way she'd come, listening to the newscast and hip-hop song fade into the quiet of the rustling forest. But then she heard another sound, the rhythm of footsteps.

At first she thought they were her own footsteps echoing in the quiet. But then she heard different distinct footfalls, and realized they didn't match her gait. Probably residents of the campground out for a stroll, but some irrational fear prevented her from turning to look. She heard men's voices, casually conversing, growing louder. Were they walking faster? They were almost behind her. She walked to the side, a little closer to the woods, and stopped to let them pass. There were three of them.

They didn't pass.

They didn't come after her either. They just stood in a semicircle and stared at her in a way that made her uncomfortable. She knew they were some of the miners Will had warned her about in town. *Keep away from them. They're not the Southern gentlemen you're used to.* They were dirty, perhaps returning home from work. Two of them smoked cigarettes. She stared back, trying to appear assertive, and then remembered Will warning her not to look at them. She looked at the cigarettes instead, glowing red pinpoints of light in the gathering darkness, and cold, sickly fear seeped into her veins. She was too far from the quiet street to call for help. She had the sinking feeling that would only bring more men.

She turned and started to walk again. Long ago, she'd read an article about how to prevent rape. *Swing your arms and hold your head high. Look assertive, and rapists will seek out an easier target.* Anyway, who was to say they meant her harm? Maybe they thought she was a prostitute out trolling for business.

Either way, she felt the metal taste of panic in her mouth. She kept walking, and they kept following. "Miss?" one of the men said, and she ignored him. He said it again, louder, with a thick accent. "Miss? Girl? Hullo."

"Hello," she muttered over her shoulder. They kept pace with her no matter how fast she walked. A moment later one of them lurched ahead of her, cutting off any chance of forward egress. A thought crystalized in her mind, or perhaps an image. A slender plane of glinting separation, a hair-thin veneer between civilization and wildness, between man and animal. It was such a thin line, but she'd never realized until now how tenuous it could be. Here, now, it slipped away until there was no line at all. She backed toward the woods, considering options. Scream, and hope they backed off? Run into the forest and hope to lose them? She didn't want to be in the woods with three men chasing her. At least on the road, there was a chance someone would see her and help her.

One of the men, the tallest one with deep-set gray eyes, walked closer. He stood in front of her and reached for a lock of her hair. "Don't," she said with as much authority as she could muster. "I have to get back. My friend is expecting me. He'll be looking for me." She babbled on, not even knowing if they spoke English.

She tried to duck around the man in front of her and they all closed in. She stopped thinking then, and operated on pure fear. *Please don't let them kill me.* She wished she were braver, that she had the balls to kick and rant and send them running, but what if it didn't work? She was afraid this scenario only ended one way, and it wasn't them inviting her to share a smoke and a hand of poker. She berated herself to fight, to run, whatever she had to do, but she was frozen. Then the men turned and Charlotte saw Will's SUV barreling toward them, trailing a cloud of dust. He braked hard, sending gravel flying in a sound Charlotte was sure she'd remember all her life.

He was out of the car and stalking toward them before she could wrap her mind around his timely arrival. "Hey, Charlotte. Come on." His voice sounded strained and his movements exaggerated. He reminded her of the way a cat puffed up when it was about to fight—but a fight here wouldn't be fair. She pushed past the men and none of them tried to stop her. She thought she saw a hint of amusement in the tall one's eyes.

"We only wish to greet her," he said in English with a sardonic bow of his head.

Will said something sharp in Adyghe, and the man returned a testy reply as Charlotte scrambled into the passenger seat and buckled herself in with shaking fingers. Her heart pounded in her chest, from terror or relief or some heady combination of the two. Will got in beside her and swung the car around in a squealing cloud of gravel and dust.

"Jesus Christ, Charlotte," he hissed as he drove. "Jesus fucking Christ. Seriously?"

"I wanted to walk." She couldn't look at him. Her palms were pools of sweat sliding across the upholstery. She clutched her hands together in her lap, refusing to cry, not while he was berating her.

"Don't go anywhere, ever," he yelled. "Don't go anywhere without me. You're the only goddamn female within ten kilometers of here."

"I didn't know. You never told me that."

"What the fuck? You don't leave a note that you're going off God knows where?"

"I wanted to walk for a while. See the scenery."

"You almost got a fucking eyeful of scenery just now, you bloody idiot. Don't go anywhere without me. Ever. Do you understand?"

"Yes, I understand. Stop cussing at me."

She wouldn't cry. She wouldn't let him see her cry, even though she wanted nothing more than to curl up in a ball and cry for hours. When they were almost to the cabin, numbness turned to alarm. "Do they know where we live? I don't want to stay at the cabin anymore. What if they come here after me?"

"They won't come."

"How do you know?"

"They're not predators. That's the way all the local men act toward women. If you're alone, without a relative or chaperone, you're fair game. They thought..." He stopped and slid a look at her bare legs. "God only knows what they thought. They figured it was their lucky night."

Charlotte's stomach wrenched. "That's sick. I was walking down the road minding my own business."

"That cultural perspective doesn't fly here, as much as you wish it did. You're being an ugly American again."

"Ugly American?" She sputtered, feeling rage. "Are you saying what they did is fine? What, I'm not considering their perspective?"

"Of course I'm not saying that. Calm down and listen to me. We are the strangers here, you and me. This is their world, their cultural point of view."

As soon as he pulled into the clearing and stopped the car, Charlotte jumped out. She turned on him when he came after her. "You should have told me. Why didn't you tell me?"

"I did. I told you in town. I tried to send you home, remember? You refused."

"You never said I wouldn't be able to go anywhere. I didn't realize—"

"What? That you couldn't stumble around doing stupid idiot-tourist shit?"

"Oh, okay. I'm an idiot tourist. I see."

"Charlotte—"

He reached for her, his voice softening, but she evaded his touch and stormed through the front door. "I want to go home. It's disgusting here."

"I told them you were my wife. They probably won't bother you again."

"They *probably* won't? That's comforting."

"They won't if you use your fucking brain."

"So this was all my fault?"

"Partly, yes. If you're going to sashay down a deserted road by yourself into a ghetto full of sex-starved men looking like that—" He gestured toward her in a blunt motion.

She narrowed her eyes. "Looking like what?"

"The way you look! With that body and those eyes, and that fucking hair, then yes, it's your fault." She stilled at his words, flung at her like epithets. He crossed his arms over his chest and stared past her, over her shoulder. "I mean, Jesus Christ. Use some common sense."

Oh, she'd use some common sense all right. "I'm going home. Right now," she said. "I'm not staying here one more night."

"Fine," he said, throwing his arms up. "Then go home. Better late than never. This wouldn't have happened if you'd fucking listened to me in the first place." He poked a vicious finger in the air. "Go pack your bags, right now, and I'll drive you to the airport."

"Fine, I will," Charlotte screamed back. She slammed the door so hard the rafters rattled. Alone in her room, the tears finally exploded, choking her, blurring her vision so all she could do for long moments was lean back against the door gasping for breath. She stuffed her fist in her mouth, not wanting him to hear. She wanted her mother. She wanted her condo. She wanted Roger's shoulder to cry on. She would never, ever complain about her boring, sheltered life again.

When she was calm enough to think, she moved to the bed and clicked on the lamp beside it. She knelt down and yanked her luggage from underneath, only to see a massive spider scuttle out and dart past her knee. She fell back, scooting on hands and knees until she hit the wall. She drew her legs up and watched the spider begin a leisurely trek up the front wall before it disappeared into a crack at the top. She looked around, paranoid. There might be more behind her. In her bed. In her hair. In the armoire with her clothes. Were there more in her suitcase? She started to cry again, a dry, aching wave of grief for all the stupid choices she'd ever made, this one being the stupidest of all.

Still, she muffled her sobs with her palms. She didn't want him to hear.

* * * * *

Will waited, looking over the notes they'd abandoned only a couple hours before. It was impossible to work, but he was trying, because the only other thing to do was think about her on the side of that road. If he'd been ten minutes later. Five minutes. If he'd stayed and looked at condoms five minutes longer...

"Charlotte," he called out, looking at his watch. "What are you doing in there?"

Silence. All he heard was silence. He knew she wasn't packing, in the same way he hoped she knew he hadn't really been angry with her.

At himself, yes. He was disgusted with himself at the moment. He typed a few more sentences and bit his lip.

"Are you okay in there?" His voice sounded loud and strange in the face of her utter silence. He knew she was still there. He'd heard her in the bathroom earlier. Heard the water run and run. He felt helpless and ugly in a way he'd never felt before. He should have made her go home. He should make her go now. They could be at the airport in Krasnodar before midnight.

"Charlotte?" *At least let me know you're okay, because I don't know how to fix you if you aren't.* "Charlotte, I have chocolate."

To his relief, her clipped voice sounded through the door. "Chocolate isn't going to make me feel better."

"I think we both know that's not true. It's yours if you'd just come out."

Her bedroom door opened with a soft, slow creak. She stood in a tee and rumpled sweatpants, a towel wrapped around her shoulders beneath a wet mass of riotous locks. She stared at the floor in front of her.

"I want you to cut my hair."

It took a moment for the words to make sense. When they did, something twisted inside him. "Like hell. Absolutely not."

"I can do the front," she said tightly. "But I need you to do the back."

"I won't do it, and I'll hide the scissors if you mention it again. I won't help you. No."

"Please." Her ragged voice was like a knife in his chest. "Please, Will. I'm not kidding."

He sighed and shut his laptop, leaning on it to study her.

"Why do you want to cut your hair?"

He knew why, but she wouldn't say it. She made some careless, false gesture of aggravation. "I can't even get a brush through it. Do you know what it's like to wash hair like this in a bathtub?"

"I would rather you stop bathing than cut it off."

Her stolid front started to crumble. She whined in a fair approximation of a three-year-old. "There's a big knot in the back."

"Well, brush it."

"I can't! It's too tangled." Then she was bawling, leaning against the doorsill like her heart was breaking. He didn't go to her the way he knew he should. He was afraid of her backing away from him with that look in her eyes. His hands clenched and unclenched under the table. He was a big, dumb, helpless male, with no idea how to help.

"Fuck's sake," he said. "Bring me your brush."

She stared at him through bleary eyes. "What?"

"If you can't untangle your hair, I'll do it for you. Bring me your brush."

He thought she might refuse, or continue to stand there crying, but she disappeared into the room. Will unwrapped the chocolate, breaking it into bite-sized pieces until Charlotte reappeared a moment later with a wide-bristled brush in her hand.

"Sit down right here."

He turned his chair to face hers and had her sit sideways so her hair fell in a long, tangled mass in front of him. She was right, it was a mess. He took a bunched-up skein from the side and started working out the snarls as gently as he could.

"Don't yank at it," she said over her shoulder.

"I'm going to pull it as hard as possible. While I'm at it, have some chocolate."

She turned frontward again with a tsk, but she did reach over to take a piece.

"What happened today, Charlotte... It wasn't your fault."

He saw her tense, saw the small lift in her shoulders. "You said it was."

"I shouldn't have. I only said that because I was angry at myself. At them." He wanted to say more, but couldn't find the words he needed. So he just said, "I'm sorry. I was wrong."

She turned her head so the brush snagged a tangle. "Ouch!"

"If you don't want it pulled, sit still. Honestly, it's a rat's nest."

Will took his time separating each tangle, and pushed the completed sections forward over her left shoulder. After a few moments, her whole body shuddered in a sigh.

"I don't know what I'm doing here. I had a perfectly safe, happy life where I was. Family and friends. Places to go. Things to do. Now I'm living out here in the middle of nowhere, with no shower—"

"You know what?" He brandished the brush over her shoulder. "Plenty of people manage to subsist in the world without showers."

"With spiders though? Big hairy spiders? I don't understand why this work is so important to you."

"You want to know why it's important? Because once upon a time, cultures all over the world worshipped women." He tapped her pile of notes with a clunk of the wooden brush. "Gods and goddesses. In the ancient mythology of this region, the earth was a woman, created by a woman. The gods were women, feared, treasured, revered. Now you've got men who feel perfectly entitled to drag you into the woods for the crime of making eye contact. You tell me why it's important."

She hissed as he caught a knot hard. "All right. Jesus."

"What if they were your words in that book?" he asked, handing her another piece of chocolate. "Your stories of love and life, and humanity? You don't have to stay, Charlotte. You probably shouldn't. But you asked why, and that's why. I think those stories are important. We can publish a book about them and share their themes with the greater world, and remind people that things weren't always the way they are now."

She flinched as he pulled another knot. "I don't really want to leave. I was upset before."

"It's okay if you want to."

"I understand now about the ugly American thing. It makes me angry, but I can't change an entire culture. From now on, I just won't go anywhere without you."

"I think that would be wise."

"So I can stay?"

"That's your call."

"Do you want me to stay?"

Will gazed at the ever-increasing expanse of smooth, feminine neck as he flipped another finished section forward. "Of course I want you to stay," he said. The temptation was overwhelming. The temptation to lean closer, to press a soft, lingering kiss at her nape. He paused, his resolve faltering. Just one kiss. He reached to brush aside an errant strand—

"You're a pretty good hair brusher."

He stopped with his lips mere inches from the curve of her shoulder. *Stop. Not tonight of all nights.* He cleared his throat and refocused on detangling. "I grew up with four little sisters. I know how to brush hair."

"Four little sisters?" She chuckled. "That's where you learned to be so mean."

"Mean? I'm not mean. I don't know where you got the idea I was mean," he said, intentionally pulling one of the last tangled strands.

"Ouch! God, Will." Her drawled protest sounded enough like the old Charlotte to put most of his fears to rest. He tugged again, just for good measure.

"Stop. I can do the rest myself." She turned and tried to wrestle the brush away from him. He pulled it up and away, out of her reach.

"One more minute and I'll be done. Sit still."

"Give it to me."

He ignored her, turning her with a hand on her shoulder. She finally capitulated with an irritated snort.

"What do you miss most about home?" he asked as he unraveled the last of her hair. "Something you wish you could have right now?"

"A sho—"

"Besides a shower," he interrupted impatiently.

She thought a long moment, tapping her fingers on the edge of her chair in a nervous tic he was learning to live with.

"Sweet tea. Tea with just...scads of sugar in it. I don't drink it a lot, just as a guilty treat. It's cool and smooth and syrupy sweet."

Will made a face. "That sounds revolting."

"It's wonderful. Have you ever had it?"

"Erm, no. Sweet tea, eh? You know, we can get tea leaves in town, and we've plenty of sugar. Why don't you brew your own? It might cheer you up."

"Maybe I will. Maybe I'll make some, and you can try it."

"Sweets for the sweet," he said, drawing the brush down the last glossy lock of hair.

"It's stupid when you say that," she muttered around a piece of chocolate.

"You're welcome," he said.

Chapter Six:
Rest and Sweet Tea

They worked the next day, and the next. Charlotte was happy to get back into it, and happy that Will didn't make a big fuss about what had happened. In hindsight, she wasn't even sure the situation was as dire as she and Will had imagined. Perhaps she only told herself that to make herself feel better. Either way, she felt ninety-nine percent okay. She was coming to enjoy the work they were doing together, and more than that, she was getting drawn into the story she was translating.

A bold braggart of a hero, Lepsch, was the central character of the tale so far. What Will said was true. Women figured heavily into the action as creators, mothers, rulers of the forest. The characters in the tale came and went in a terribly confusing way, and Will suggested they might have been compiled as they came through oral tradition—sometimes mixed up, sometimes out of order. At the end, he said, she would see the big picture and it would all make sense.

She hoped so. By week's end, she was no longer jet-lagged and getting better at washing her hair in the bath tub. Will helped her brush it out afterward, insisted on it actually. She tried not to complain at the occasional tug. There was no more sniping and arguing, no more crises aside from a spider-in-the-toilet incident that left both of them shaken. Will declared Saturday Rest and Sweet Tea Day, and Charlotte agreed that sounded like a wonderful idea. He lured her to the lake around noon, promising to swim with his clothes on, a promise he broke as soon as she settled under a nearby tree with her stack of notes.

"Will!" she protested as he stripped off his tee shirt and khaki shorts.

"I'll leave my pants on, woman. Stop squawking."

"Your pants are right there." She pointed indignantly to his shorts on the ground.

"Those are shorts, not pants. These are pants." He indicated his tight white briefs with no modesty whatsoever.

"Those are underpants."

"Britons call them pants."

"Whatever they are, they leave nothing to the imagination. My eyes! I'm blind."

"It's no more than the good Lord gave me." He ambled down the gravelly shoreline into the shallows and dove under the water, his broad freckled back rippling in a disturbingly sexy way. Why did he have to be so hot? Why couldn't he have been some skinny, nerdy researcher, or the old, decrepit man she'd pictured before she flew over here in the first place? He bobbed up in the middle of the lake.

"Come in. The water's great."

"I'm working," she said, waving her sheaf of notes.

"You're not supposed to be working. It's Rest and Sweet Tea Day."

"And you're supposed to be swimming with your clothes on," she yelled back.

"I'm wearing my *pants*."

Charlotte laughed and turned her back on him. "Anyway," she yelled over her shoulder, "Ivo didn't tell me to bring a swimming suit."

"Because we don't wear swimming suits here. Or as civilized people call them, bathing suits. C'mon, take it all off and come in. Live a little."

"No." She bent over her notes, trying to concentrate. She heard more splashing, the sound of his body moving through the water and then climbing out. Soon he was dripping beside her.

"You're missing out, you know. Because of your prudishness."

She peered up at him, pointedly avoiding his midsection.

"A normal person doesn't strip down and go swimming totally naked. Not in public. Yes, I know," she said before he could protest again. "I am aware you're wearing pants."

He started to dry himself. "I'm not giving up my naked swims because some puritanical woman can't look at a man's parts without going blind."

She narrowed her eyes, keeping her gaze riveted to his face. "I am not puritanical."

"Yes, you are."

"Why are you so nasty?"

"Why are you so nice?" He flopped down beside her on his side, his head propped on his arm. "So very, very nice."

"It's nice to be nice. You should try it. It makes people like you."

"You like me fine the way I am." He gave her a devilish grin. She hated that he saw right through her. She grasped for chilly hauteur, for cool propriety, even if a nearly naked man was lounging beside her on a towel and smiling in the most insanely attractive way.

"I most certainly do not like you, Will Mayfair. I think you're vulgar and rude."

"I think you like me, Charlotte Rowe."

"I think you're deluded." She gave him her gravest frown. "Are you coming onto me?"

"Seems like a good time for it. My clothes are off. Except for my pants."

"Ugh."

He stood with a chuckle, and a moment later she heard his wet tighty-whities fall on the ground. Charlotte kept her eyes averted until he sat back down beside her, looking just as sexy in his faded blue tee and slouchy khaki shorts.

"All right, I'm dressed. You can breathe again," he said. He nodded at her notes. "How's it coming?"

She sorted through the ever-growing stack. "It's coming. Do you have any theories of who actually wrote this stuff?"

"It's not 'stuff.' It's a document of historical significance. The Caucasus region has spawned some of the more interesting mythological yarns."

"They do go on and on."

Will shrugged and rolled onto his back, resting his head on his sculpted forearms and gazing up at the sky. "You know how I really got hooked on this region? On all the dialects here? In this culture, they used to believe words had an almost...magic power. They used to heal their sick with stories and songs instead of medicine."

Charlotte glanced up from her papers. "Did it work?"

"It must have. They still do it today. When their children become gravely ill, they sing them lullabies encouraging them to die, in hopes they'll stubbornly gain strength and live."

Charlotte's thoughts lit up with a memory. "My grandfather used to rock me to sleep with a lullaby about staying awake. My mother said it always worked."

He slanted a grin at her. "You see? Magic."

"Or reverse psychology," Charlotte said, laughing. "You know a lot about this culture, don't you?"

"If you study the language, you learn the culture."

"My grandfather learned languages as a hobby. He didn't know as many as you, but he liked trying them out. He used to say language was the heart of humanity."

Will considered that a moment. "Maybe once. Not anymore. Money's the heart of humanity now."

"You think so? Money's not my heart."

"Because you've got plenty of it."

"How do you know that?" she asked, miffed at his reproving tone.

"Oh, come on, Charlotte. Look around you, look at this region. This is human struggle. Poverty. Real life. You've lived your privileged little existence in the American suburbs, doted on by your parents, your grandfather, utterly sheltered from the ugly side of life. You were able to start a successful business, your own business. There are places in the world where women aren't even allowed to work, or vote, or own property. You're wealthy beyond belief, believe me."

"What about you? You had an education, the opportunity to learn all those languages," she pointed out. "You don't seem destitute by any means."

"I didn't say I was. I'm saying it's easy to be offhand about money when you've had everything you've ever needed. Your defensiveness speaks volumes," he added.

"Your super judgmental idiocy speaks volumes."

"I like that," he said, rolling up onto an elbow. "I should put that on my business card. *Dr. William Mayfair, Super Judgmental Idiot.*"

"Etch it on your tombstone so everyone can remember how pleasant you were," she sniffed.

"I might, after you kill me with those poison looks."

"If you don't want poison looks, don't be so obnoxious."

They glared at each other for a long moment before Will broke first and lay back. "All right, Charlotte," he chuckled.

"Charlotte." She rolled her eyes. "Honestly, the way you say my name."

He leaned up again. "That's your name, right? Charlotte?"

"The way you say it! Dripping with derision every time." She had to try very hard not to stare at his broad chest, and the way the loose tee still managed to highlight the eloquently masculine shape of him. It was even harder to look in his deep blue eyes. In the sun, they seemed as direct and incisive as lasers. She curled her lips, tossing her hair back over one shoulder. "*Chaaar-lit*," she mimicked.

One corner of his mouth twitched up, then he turned it right back on her. "When you say my name, *Chaaar-lit*, you make it sound like a round thing on a bicycle. *Wheel.*"

She scowled. "I do not say it like that."

"I'm afraid you do."

"Will."

"See? *Wheel*. It's not *Wheel*, it's Will. *Will*. Try it."

"Will." She heard her own twang, even though she tried to stifle it. He laughed and sang out, "*Wheel, Wheel, Wheel.*"

"That's just how I talk."

"That's just how I *tawlk*."

"I'll smack you."

"I'll *smayck* you." He laughed again, a rich, jubilant sound that had her laughing too despite her aggravation. She gave him a light indignant slap. He trapped her hand and then she was falling against him, her rattling papers still clutched in one fist. "Will," she breathed, but it didn't come out as indignant as she'd hoped. His fingers spread on the back of her neck and he drew her close without even seeming to. The kiss was a whisper, achingly gentle, a brush across her lips. Then a laugh, perhaps at himself. Perhaps at the way she stiffened. He pressed his cheek to hers, and another soft laugh vibrated beside her ear.

"Bloody hell," he sighed, pulling away and lying back again.

Myriad warnings crowded through her brain at that moment, every one of them ignored. Untold generations of reserved southern forebears would have been scandalized by the way she fell on top of him. His eyes went wide, but he did nothing to stop her, only assisted in her efforts to mold her body to his. His arms tightened around her, his gaze dark and serious now. He explored her lips and neck with feathery kisses and made wonderful sounds, sighs and little growls that made her press against him harder. An ache grew and spread that called out for relief, and she thought, *this is dangerous*. And then she thought, *I don't care*.

"Will," she whispered, letting go of the papers and threading her fingers through his sun-tinged blond hair. He was so solid, so warm beneath her. Her fingers tightened, a demand as much as a plea. Their eyes met and held for a long, intense moment, and then he exploded into movement, rolling her onto her back. She vaguely registered the sound of her notes crumpling under her. He held her hands over her head as his kiss deepened and intensified. His lips slanted over hers, tasting her, urging her to respond.

She arched up against him as far as she could, which wasn't very far with him pinning her down. She could feel the outline of his cock through his khakis, through her sateen bermuda shorts. The ache turned to a pulse, and then a need that drove her to reach for him, struggling against the controlling shackles of his fingers.

"No," he whispered against her lips. "I don't want to let you go." He spread her thighs with a firm, gravel-encrusted knee, then slid over her, nudging his cock against the juncture of her thighs, against that hot, wanting place that had ached for days to be filled by him. Five years. It had been five years for her, but even longer since she'd experienced need like this. It had been forever. She'd never felt this much impassioned craving in her life. She wanted him to take her right then and there, on the dusty ground with the sun blazing over his shoulders. He was so big from her vantage point, he blocked out the mountains.

He kissed her hard, his big palms hot and damp against her arms. His fingers curled and uncurled on her wrists. As he nipped at her lips, as his tongue thrust in and teased at hers, he kept pressing...grinding. She writhed under him, and then a long, low moan escaped. If he released her hands, she would use them to rip off every shred of his clothing.

"Not here," he said, drawing away. The effort of stopping, even talking, showed in the tense lines of his face. "We have to go inside." She gave him a pleading, befuddled look. "Protection," he said sharply.

Oh, God. Yes. Protection. What was wrong with her? Thank God one of them still had a functioning brain. She managed to scoop up her crushed notes before he took her arm and dragged her toward the cabin. She wanted to push up his shirt as he strode along in front of her. She wanted to run her fingers across the warm, firm landscape of his back, and then lower, to the curve of his perfect, round ass. *No, you hussy. Wait.* No other man had ever made her feel this way, so desperately and alarmingly aroused. She was usually the one pursued. In bed, she played along. Faked it. Left things to her partner. She'd definitely never wanted to tear her lover's clothes off.

Not until now.

* * * * *

Will took her to his room. His bed was bigger, and he had condoms in the bureau. *Russian condoms*, his conscience whispered. He prayed the condoms were more dependable than his restraint. They would have to do because there was no human way he was stopping the seduction at this point.

Seduction? It wasn't even a seduction. He'd kissed her on a whim, impulsively, to see her reaction. When she'd fallen on top of him, ripe and eager, it was like falling into some alternative universe where prim Charlotte Rowe was as horny and depraved as he was. He slid a look at her as he stripped, before he crossed the room to dig out the rubbers. Depraved, perhaps not. But horny—yes. God, yes, and thank you, universe.

Charlotte stripped too. He gazed at the spectacle of her. *Goddess.* Her breasts were high and full, her hips a beckoning, feminine masterpiece. He took her down to the bed, laid on top of her skin-to-skin. He buried his head in the curve of her neck and then dropped kisses down to her lovely globes, tasting and nibbling the whole way. He still smelled like the lake, his hair damp and earthy. She smelled like the sun, fresh and clean and wonderfully female. He ran a hand down her side, gentle fingers exploring, mapping her out. Her enticing contours coaxed some wild, primal drive inside him to life. His cock surged against her, filling to almost painful hardness. He'd wanted her so badly. He hadn't taken her, because... Because... He couldn't even remember now.

His fingers slowed and his exploration grew more tentative. He slid his hand lower and parted her with careful control. If she resisted him, he would stop in an instant. He watched her as he sought the slick, swollen treasure at the apex of her mons. "Ohhhh..." she breathed. She didn't resist at all.

He would never forget her in that moment. Naked, trembling, her head thrown back and her hair arrayed like a sunburst around her. She trusted him utterly, which both pleased and perturbed him. "Charlotte," he whispered. "Are you sure?"

He still stroked her hot, wet center. He saw her blink and try to focus on his words as her hips jerked and responded to his touch. "Are you sure?" he asked again, when he thought she was managing to listen to him.

She made a lovely frustrated sound and arched against his fingers, clutching his shoulders in a response he couldn't misunderstand. He answered with his own groan and twisting hips. His cock slid against the inside of her thigh, and then against her slick center. The impulse to thrust, to join with her immediately almost crippled him. There was more to discuss. There were desires to share and assurances to give, but it would have to wait until after. He fumbled with the condom, tore away the Cyrillic-printed cellophane. He reached between their bodies to roll it onto his cock, then grasped her thigh and pulled it up, parting her legs wide.

He held himself up on one elbow, looking down between them as he pressed inside her. Ah, the delicious pressure against the head of his cock, and then the tight slide into her pussy. A tortured groan rose in his throat. She fit him perfectly, almost too perfectly. He shuddered and steeled himself to control, though he wanted to thrust in her wildly. Mark her, ravage her. He let his body fall against hers. Their hips met in a questing, seeking rhythm, and their kisses grew intense, almost savage. She made animalistic sounds of pleasure that resonated in his cock and all over his body. He could barely believe the wanton woman in his arms was the Charlotte he knew.

After all the craving, all the groveling flirtation, their joining seemed nothing less than a miracle. Too soon, long before he wanted it to end, he felt pressure building in his balls, in the base of his shaft. A tickling urge for completion. He fucked her harder, faster, driving her into the bed. He knew he was being too rough, but she didn't stop him. Rather, she grabbed his hips and dug her nails into his buttocks, urging him deeper still. His whole body vibrated, reaching for release, but he didn't want it without her. He gazed down at her in all her insatiable glory. She was biting her lower lip, tossing her head back and forth on her own reckless quest for completion. "Come on, girl. Come for me."

He wanted to feel her grasp and clench around his cock, wanted to watch her face light up in ecstasy.

"Come on," he urged her again. He filled his hand with one of her breasts, watched her chest rise and fall beneath him as if her breath was his own breath. He ran his thumb over the tip and then closed his fingers on it, pinching until she reacted. Her eyes flew to his and he saw a message there. He dipped his head and bit her nipple harder, worrying the pink tip between his teeth. She dug fingers into his hips, then scratched them up his back. "Harder," she rasped. Her legs curled around him as she arched to him in a frantic movement. "Oh, God, please!"

He cupped her bottom in his hands and drove into her, feeling an intensity, a connection he'd never felt with any bed partner before. Her ragged cry sounded against his ear like music. He held her close and felt the moment her orgasm took over. He wanted to enjoy the sight of her pleasure, the rough sounds she made, but his own orgasm shook him apart in an instant. He shuddered and closed his eyes, letting the pleasure turn him inside out while he breathed in her scent. He came to rest, still drawn up tight with the aftershocks of his climax. She lay motionless. Slowly her fingers unwound from his back.

When he could move again he leaned down and cupped her face. "Just think," he whispered. "We haven't even gotten to the sweet tea yet."

She opened her eyes and blinked, as if seeing him for the first time. It pained him that she looked horrified. "Oh, no. Oh…no… Why did we do this?"

Not the words he'd wanted to hear. Some shutter inside him banged closed as he pulled away to deal with the condom. Anger flared, erasing the previous moment's pleasure. *Don't regret this, Charlotte. Damn you.* By the time he was back, she was sitting up, all but shrinking away from him.

"Jesus Christ, Charlotte. What?"

"You planned this the whole time," she said in bitter accusation. "Rest and Sweet Tea Day? Please."

"Oh, I planned this? You've wanted me from the moment you saw me."

"I did not."

"Did too. Anyway, you started it, not me."

"You kissed me first."

"Right, and then I lay down on the ground and next thing I knew, you were straddling me."

She gasped in outrage. "I've never straddled a man in my life!"

"Somehow I believe that," he snapped. They were cruel words, a terrible thing to say to a woman who'd just treated him to the most intense sex of his life. He spread his arms, hating this moment. "Okay, I'm sorry you have regrets. But you can't tell me you didn't enjoy what we just did. That you didn't want it."

She blinked again, in full prim-puritan mode, then got up to throw her clothes back on. "Fine, I enjoyed it, but it's not happening again."

Will stepped into his shorts with a doubtful snort.

"It's not," she snapped.

"I'm guessing at least twice more before you stumble off to bed insisting you didn't want it."

"You're so wrong." She went into the bathroom and slammed the door, only to emit a shrill scream a moment later.

"Throw something at it," Will yelled at the wall between them.

He heard a bang and more screams. "Did you get it?"

"I stabbed it with your toothbrush." She ran the water for a while. He waited in her room until she stormed through from the other side. She squared off with him, her arms crossed over her chest.

He jabbed a finger at her. "You promised me sweet tea, you ornery vixen, and I'm holding you to it."

She made a noise of frustration. "Do you think this is funny?"

"I think you're overreacting. It was great sex. What's the problem?"

"The problem is I don't do stuff like this. I don't. I can't. Don't ask me to, please."

The *please* killed him. "Charlotte—"

"No. No 'Charlotte.' Promise me."

He looked at her, wishing he knew the right words to say. Wishing he knew why she was pushing him away so hard. "Did I hurt you?" he asked in a low, flat voice. "Was I too rough? I thought you were enjoying it."

Her lips twisted as she rubbed her forehead. "I was enjoying it."

"Then what?"

"Ugh. You don't understand. My last few relationships— They cheated on me and...oh, God, I can't explain, just—"

"Wait. I thought you weren't in a relationship."

"I'm not. That's the point. I did a lot of thinking after my last relationship ended and I made some decisions about respecting myself and *protecting* myself. I know you think I'm being prissy and controlling. But, please...this is not my thing."

"Fine, of course," he conceded a bit curtly. "Whatever you like. I think it's silly though. We could have a lot of fun here together while we pass the time. A *lot* of fun."

She twisted her fingers together and gave a small shrug that effectively dismissed the idea. "Do you really want that sweet tea? I'll make it if you want it."

He gazed at her for a long moment, wanting much more than sweet tea. Damn. He'd called this situation the very first day.

"I'm dying for some tea, Charlotte," he said. "If tea is all I can have, that's what I want. Make it for me, please."

* * * * *

Charlotte puttered around the kitchen, not wanting to ask about the things she didn't know. She couldn't look at him without blushing, and the way he looked back at her...

Sex with him had been astonishing, passionate and amazing, which was why they couldn't ever do it again. Yes, she wanted sex as much as he did, but she'd made a promise to herself to guard her self esteem. To protect her heart from being broken—again. Most of all, she'd pledged to refrain from casual sex, even with guys as hot as Will Mayfair.

Especially with guys like him. If he left her—wait—*when* he left her—she couldn't deal with the fall out. And he would leave when all of this was over. So would she.

Therefore, no more sex with him. No. Her curiosity was assuaged; that had to be enough. She made the self-protective decision to focus all her energy and attention on the tea. Rest and Sweet Tea Day, he'd said. What a load of bullshit—but it was either make tea or risk falling back into bed with him.

The problem was, she wasn't sure how many tea leaves she needed or how long it should steep. Back in Savannah, she'd gone to the store and bought sweet tea in plastic gallon jugs, or at least brewed tea from neatly pre-packed tea bags. She didn't want to admit to him that she'd never made tea from scratch, especially after his lecture about her cushy life.

As she pondered and puttered, she could feel his eyes on her back, but then she'd turn and he'd be looking intently at his computer screen. Porn? She could very well imagine him with a serious porn habit. If his bedroom skills were any indication, he knew a lot about the art of lovemaking. Not that what they'd done together had felt anything like art, or lovemaking. More like uncontrolled, unadulterated...porn.

"Oww." She hissed as she singed the tip of a finger on the pan of boiling water. She was pretty sure the outmoded stove and cookware were twice as old as her. She thought the liquid looked dark amber enough to make workable tea. It was perhaps a bit too dark, so she diluted it with some water from the sink. She looked around for the sugar bowl only to yelp as he materialized beside her with it.

"Sweets for the sweet."

"God," she said under her breath, grabbing it from him. "You scared me to death." She started dumping sugar into the tea as he looked on in fascination. "Go ahead," she muttered.

"What?"

"Say something about how revolting it's going to taste."

"Revolting...probably. I'm more worried about my teeth rotting."

"Don't knock it if you haven't tried it."

"I knock it, Miss Sugar." He turned away, mumbling something under his breath about his toothbrush and stabbed spiders as she put two glasses on the counter. She gave the tea an assessing glance. "It should probably cool off for awhile."

"I know a way we could pass the time."

Charlotte shook her head firmly. "No. I'll use ice."

"Erm...ice?"

"There's no ice?"

"Have you had ice even one time since you've been here?"

"Well, no, but there's always ice in freezers." She flung open the freezer door, flabbergasted at the lack of ice cube trays.

"Ice is an American thing," said Will.

She gave him a dire look. "If you call me an ugly American again, I'll kick you square in the nuts with every ounce of my strength."

Will held up his hands in a gesture of surrender. Charlotte grabbed the pan of tea and moved to dump it in the sink.

"Stop, stop, stop," he said, diving for the handle. "Don't."

"It's useless without ice. That's the whole point of it. It's supposed to be cool and refreshing."

"We'll drink it warm then, and pretend it's cold."

"Forget it. No."

"Wait...stop. Let me." He tipped the warm tea into the two glasses. "Come on, let's go drink it on the porch."

With a frown, she followed him out, grabbing two spoons on the way. No ice? Ridiculous. Back home she was always on top of everything, but it seemed she couldn't do anything right here. She stirred her tea glumly, the spoon clinking against the side of her glass, then handed a spoon to him. "You have to spin it, or the sugar collects on the bottom."

"That doesn't tell you something? Like maybe you used too much sugar?"

She ignored his sniping, taking a sip of the lukewarm mixture. What she'd created was close, but not the real thing. A dialect. Will hesitated, then took a sip of his.

Followed by an exaggerated spit-take.

"For God's sake," she said, turning to go inside. He stopped her with a hand on her arm.

"I was kidding. It was a joke."

Charlotte felt dangerously close to tears. How silly, to get upset about some stupid joke of his, when the stupid jokes never ended. How silly to fall head over heels for a man she'd only just met, and have amazing sex with him, so every time he came near her now she felt an excruciating physical ache. She kept her gaze fixed on the distant mountains. "I know we were supposed to rest today," she said. "But I'd rather get back to work." Again, she started inside.

"It's actually not so bad. Now that I give it a chance."

She turned to him. He took another tentative sip. She could tell he suppressed a grimace.

"Please stop drinking it. You hate it."

"I don't hate it."

"You certainly don't like it."

He stroked his glass, his gaze traveling over her for a slow, thoughtful moment. "To be honest, I don't know what to think of it yet."

Chapter Seven: Folie à deux

They didn't have another Rest and Sweet Tea Day, although the memory of his lovemaking lingered and haunted her, especially in her bed at night.

Will acted the consummate gentleman, never mentioning her complete loss of control or the fact that, yes, it had been her fault things had gone way beyond his playful kiss. She knew she'd hurt his feelings when she withdrew from him afterward, but the whole thing had scared her. She could envision them doing it again and again...and again... They might never leave the bedroom, and Charlotte hadn't come here to get her freak on. She'd come here to save a dialect, to finish in a timely manner and go back home.

During the day they worked in the tight confines of the antiquities storage room, her knee bumping his with annoying regularity. He pretended not to notice. With her rejection of him as a lover, he settled into the role of researcher with an even more focused intensity. The awful thing was, his brainy-insightful-linguist persona was a hundred times hotter than his flirtatious-cad persona. She picked at her white cotton gloves, watching him turn the time-worn pages of the book with a reverence that undid her. Each page that turned was a relief to her. One page closer to flying home again, away from all this temptation.

In the evenings it was even more difficult, because in the evenings there were beds just a few steps away from where they worked. She would argue silently with herself. *What would it hurt? A little empty sex, that's all. Why is that such a threat to you?*

Because I'm tired of emotional pain, her mind would answer, *and Will Mayfair and I have no future.* In fact, he irritated her like crazy. The only reason they'd hooked up was because they were stuck together in the middle of nowhere... *And because he's completely, sinfully hot.*

Tonight they sat over their notes as they did every night. Around eight, as always, he got up and made coffee so they could press on another couple hours. He returned with coffee cups and the sugar bowl, pushing it over to her.

"Sweet for the sweet."

"It drives me nuts when you say that."

"I know. That's why I do it."

She wanted to slap the grin off his face every bit as much as she wanted to kiss him. She ignored the coffee and sugar, and started to tap her pencil on the table. He gave her an annoyed look and she stopped. He took a long, slow slurp of his inky brew. It was like nails across a chalkboard.

"Jesus," she said under her breath.

Will put his cup down with a bang. "You know, people who live alone with each other day in and day out start to suffer from a certain type of mental illness. *Folie à deux.* The madness of two."

"That's fascinating."

"Symptoms include frustration, hostility, violence—" His hand came down on her tapping pencil with enough force to break it. "And insanity. If you do not stop that tapping I will kill you."

"You broke my pencil."

"You're breaking my brain."

They bickered. Every night they bickered. He was right, they were driving one another down the path to insanity. She took the two pieces of her pencil and flung them at his head, missing to the right side.

"You're the one who slurps coffee every evening like some kind of drunken tree frog."

"Drunken tree frog? Frogs don't slurp, they ribbit, princess. You never kissed one?"

"I told you to stop calling me princess! And don't tell me what frogs say. I don't give a fucking damn about frogs. Stop slurping your damn coffee."

His eyes narrowed as he shoved his cup away. "Enough, okay? Seriously, we're going to argue about frogs? Why don't you give in already? Put both of us out of our misery?"

"I don't know what you're talking about," she said, her eyes riveted on her notes.

"You know bloody well what I'm talking about, *princess*."

She gritted her teeth against her body's own weakness, her own desire. "We discussed this days ago. It was a mistake."

"You felt it was a mistake. I enjoyed it immensely and would very much like to do it again."

"Well, I wouldn't."

"That's a lie. You're a silly little liar, Charlotte."

She made a wild, inarticulate noise of aggravation and turned her back on him. "I'm trying to work. Can we please just work and let go of the other stuff?"

The other stuff. Will's heat and virility, the hard perfection of his body covering hers. His breath blowing across her lips and his hands holding her down with such ardent power...

She hunched over her papers, trying to refocus on the dancing villagers who were wishing their warrior-traveler a farewell. A send off. God, why did the words all have so many possible translations? A moment later she saw a new pencil slide across the table.

"Thank you," she ground out.

"Try not to tap it." He thrust a page under her nose. "What's this word?"

She looked down at the word he pointed to with his rough masculine fingers, those fingers that had done such wonderful things to her. "Like...what do you call those things blacksmiths use?"

"A hammer? A mallet?"

"No, like..." She pinched her fingers together, meeting his intent blue eyes.

"Tongs?"

"I don't know what they're called. Pinchers or tongs? Blacksmiths use them. He's a blacksmith."

"I thought he was a warrior."

"He's a warrior, but he makes his own weapons."

Will frowned and scrawled some notes before returning to his laptop. "Could you be a bit clearer in your word choices? This will go faster if you do."

"It isn't easy, you know. A lot of this translation is complicated."

"Complicated how? You take one language and write it in another. You're the one making it complicated. I've told you, pick the best choice and go with it."

"You're the one complaining that I have to be clearer."

"Charlotte—"

"A lot of these words have double meanings. I don't want to get too far from the original. Have you ever translated anything before? I'd like to see you—"

"Shh."

Her eyes widened. "Did you just shush me?"

"You're yammering. It's annoying."

"If I'm so annoying, Dr. Critical, maybe you should get someone else to translate for you."

"Maybe I should."

She squelched the urge to throw another pencil at him—or something heavier. A boulder, maybe. A pair of tongs. "You always do that."

"Do what?"

"'*Maybe I should.*' Shut up is what you really mean."

"Yes, that is what I mean."

She turned to him and stood, about to unload a hammerful of pissed-off-southern-girl on his head, but he grabbed her first and pressed a kiss to her lips.

She shoved at him. "You know what—"

He silenced her with another forceful kiss. Her hands crept up to thread in his hair of their own volition.

"Will—"

Again he kissed her, his tongue and lips overtaking hers, melting her resistance. Damn him. She forgot what she'd been so angry about in the first place. Tongs. Translation. Boulder... *Will.* She pushed him away with all the force of her denied lust for him.

"Why did you do that?" she asked, dragging a hand across her lips.

"To shut you up."

"God, I'll be happy to shut up if you never do that aga—"

His next kiss took her breath away. Sensuous, insistent, impassioned.

"Ohhh." She moaned against his lips, not a sound of protest but a sound of entreaty. She'd tried to resist him, but she'd known all along it would come to this. Chaos, and the revelation that the pull between them was stronger than either of their wills. She drew away, forcing herself to relinquish her grasp on his shirt. "We should get back to work."

"I'm done working for the moment."

"We shouldn't."

"Yes, we should. Jesus, Charlotte, I want you so badly. Don't you want me too?" He whispered against her lips, pleas and promises she couldn't resist. He took her hand and the smallest pressure had her following him to the bedroom. Words of mythology drifted through her mind, in English and Adyghe. *Lady Satanay said, go roam the mountains and plains. See how other people live, and learn their secrets. Bring back knowledge. Search to the ends of the earth.* "It's okay. It's okay," he said as he pushed her back on the bed. "Isn't it?"

"Oh, God," she whispered. "Yes. Okay." It wasn't organized or advisable, or any of those things Charlotte valued so highly, but she couldn't make herself care. She pushed off his shirt and pulled at his waistband as he slid his fingers under her top and pulled it off. He stopped her, peeling her hands from the rigid staff rising out of his shorts.

"Wait. Slower this time."

She shook her head, but his hand closed around her wrist and held it hard. "I don't want it to be over quickly," he insisted. "This time, I want to explore you." *Learn their secrets. Bring back knowledge.*

Will started with kisses, lingering slow caresses along her jaw and down her neck. He licked along the top of her breasts, warm, wet pressure, sliding one hand beneath her to draw her closer. By the time he tugged down the cups of her bra to blow on her nipples, she was ready to combust.

"Please," she begged. But he wasn't like her other lovers. He took his time, took over her body like it was his toy to play with. When she said it again, "Please," he brushed her hair back and gave her a patient look, just as he moved his hips to tease her a little. She could feel the tip of his cock poking her through his clothes, and her clothes. It was only a hint of the thick, invading pleasure she remembered from last time. With Will, everything felt primal. She ached for him like an animal, not a polite, civilized woman.

"Please," she asked one more time. She could have taken her own pants off. Physically, she could have. Mentally, she was enslaved by his stare and the possessive touch of his fingers holding her down. He took off her bra and played some more with her nipples, biting and licking them, mixing pain and pleasure while she clung to his shoulders and thrust her hips forward. Finally, he slid a hand down and undid the front of her shorts. She shimmied them off along with her panties, and pulled again at his waistband. He stayed her hand with a sharp sound.

"Lie back and be good," he whispered. "Or I might have to tie you down."

She believed he would do it. Part of her wanted him to do it, wanted him to take this sensual control a step further. She had known from the start he wasn't like other men. There was something simmering inside him that the other men she'd been with lacked. He was stronger, more volatile, more *vital*. He was like Lepsch, the dashing hero of the mythology on his quest. He had no doubts, no reasonable caution, just a driving desire to explore and conquer.

He groped between her thighs and parted her pussy lips, pressing through slickness and moisture, teasing her precisely where she craved to be touched. He was silent but she wanted words, assurances. Without words, what they were doing felt too intense and too threatening. She tried to speak. "Will—" But he cut off her voice with a deep, aggressive kiss. His hand, still wet with her essence, threaded in her hair and pulled. With his other hand, he held her thighs open against all her instincts to draw them closed.

When he left her mouth and lowered himself to her pussy, she fought him in earnest. It wasn't that she didn't like oral sex. In fact, she loved it. But she knew, instinctively, that Will's brand of oral wouldn't be the polite stimulation of her past lovers. The first hint was the way he held her down, his arms wrapped around her legs.

"No, please—"

"Oh, yes," he sighed. Against her struggling, against the frantic bucking of her hips, he took her with his mouth. He lapped at her, bringing sensation to a fever peak, then nipped at the insides of her labia. He held her open with his fingers and nibbled on her clit. The rush of arousal was immediate, overwhelming. Her whole pelvis throbbed with a shivering desire to climax as her moans grew to an embarrassing volume. She was falling, completely losing herself to the insistence of her need. His tongue flicked and teased her, playing over nerve endings that screamed for more and more pleasure. It was almost too much to bear, but his wide shoulders wouldn't allow her legs to close. She clutched his hair and pulled hard, a last ditch effort at regaining some control. He let her pull, then grabbed her hips and flipped her over onto her stomach, pinning her wrists to the bed. Somehow he managed to kick off his shorts as she lay there under him, sucking in air.

His erection poked against the juncture of her thighs as he shifted on top of her, nuzzling his cheek against hers. She was shaking, so horny and yet so panicked. It was happening again, the complete loss of control, the loss of herself to their joining. His sibilant shushing noises joined the hum in her clit and the dull ache in her nipples, one overwhelming white noise of craving in her brain. She couldn't even say *please* anymore, couldn't even beg him. She felt caught in some quagmire of his making.

"Stay," he said, and she stayed while he left to sheathe himself. She knew it was for her protection, even if it felt like torture to lie there without his weight calming her and bearing her down. Her pussy was so wet. She remembered, like yesterday, the girth and length of him filling her, and she shuddered in anticipation of feeling that again. The bed dipped and his hands were on her thighs again, grasping, parting. He slid a palm beneath her and gave a sharp command. "Up."

She struggled to her hands and knees, to the unfamiliar, carnal position. *Please, please, please, please...* She heard the whimpered words in the darkness and realized they were coming from her. Again the soft shushing and the hard demand of his touch. One hand splayed on her waist, pulling her back against him, while the other grabbed a fistful of hair. She felt the nudge of his cock at her slit. He slid inside, then out. She whined and wiggled her hips back against him, needing more, needing all of it. The hand in her hair tightened, and a low dangerous voice rasped at her ear.

"Admit it. Out loud. You want this."

Yes, I want it. God help me, I want it so bad. "Yes," she said. "Yes."

"You've wanted this since the last time. It was good, wasn't it? We're good together."

"Yes!" She dropped her head, admitting what she hadn't wanted to. "Yes, we're good together."

"Say it," he prompted. "'I want you to fuck me.'"

He would make her beg. She deserved it. She swallowed hard and said the words. "I want you to fuck me. Please."

Charlotte moaned as he entered her. She could feel the quivering restraint in the way he held her, in the deliberate way he slid in her, this time all the way to the hilt. From somewhere within, a purr unwound and lingered. He held her trapped on his cock, impaled to the very center of her being. Her walls clenched around his hard length and he groaned. "You see, Charlotte?" he said. "You see?"

He began to move, not waiting for her answer. Oh yes, she saw. She understood. If not for his hand bracing her, she would have collapsed flat on the bed. Her knees were jelly, and her arousal was rising at a breakneck pace toward an apex. His cock was the driving, physical manifestation of his power. He released her hair and grabbed her hips, taking her with sure strokes. One hand snaked down and slid over her clit, rough touches and then tender taps, both of them feeding the ache inside her. Her shoulders fell forward as the pace of his strokes quickened. She met him in her own way, pressing back to take him deep. As her orgasm neared, her hips took on a wild rhythm. She looked over her shoulder at him kneeling behind her, a fierce, passionate male having his way with her. He slid a hand up her spine and clasped the back of her neck. His fingers tightened and something inside her responded to his force.

The climax was blinding. The tension between her legs released into throbbing waves along every nerve of her body. She arched and clamped down on his cock, each fluttering contraction around his hard tool an unbearable delight. A moment later, his hands tightened on her hips and he bore her down, down, down into the softness of the bed with punishing thrusts. She experienced it all in some post-orgasmic state of bliss, felt his wrenching shout and shudder as if from somewhere far away. He collapsed over her, his ribs pressing against her back. He stroked her hair and pressed warm, soft kisses against her temple, then laid his head over hers.

Slowly, as the sex haze ebbed away, Charlotte's mind caught up to her traitorous body. *How? Why?* Questions she didn't have an answer for. Why did it work this way between them? She'd barely known him a month, and he wasn't her type. Annoying, irresponsible, disorganized. How could he cast this spell and conquer her like some ancient god-warrior, when all she wanted was to resist him? Why must his cock feel so perfect, even now, resting inside her? Why did the tickle of his hair against her cheek feel so right? She took a shuddery breath, trying to stuff down all the confusing emotions inside her.

In the midst of her thoughts, he found her hand and curled his fingers around it, threading them through hers. *Oh, no. This is so risky. This is so dangerous.* She couldn't stop herself from pulling her hand away. She scooted from under him while he took off the condom.

"No," he said. "Don't do this. Not again."

"I need to be alone for a…a minute. No offense."

He beat her to the door, leaning against it so she couldn't leave. She looked up at him warily.

"Please, Will. This is messing me up." She meant to say something firmer and more assertive. Why were her language skills deserting her now? It was as if she sacrificed them for the Adyghe dialect she was keeping from extinction. Even as she grasped for words to shut him out, she let him take her in his arms, cup her face and smooth her hair back.

"Really?" he asked. "You want me to leave you alone?"

"Yes."

"Was it that bad? I thought it was…" He cast about for words. Her own mind filled them in. *Amazing. Earth-shattering. Terrifying.*

"It was great," she said. "But I can't deal with casual sex, I told you that. It feels wrong to me. A little painful. After."

There was an awkward silence, where she wished to hear him say six simple words. *It wasn't casual sex to me.* She wanted to hear him say something to refute her. But he didn't.

"I'll try to leave you alone," he said instead. "If that's what you want. But you don't make it easy." His gaze was sad, angry.

He opened the door for her, and after she left, slammed it behind her with a bang.

Chapter Eight:
Circassian Beauties

The next day, they stayed at the library transcribing until the attendant closed the doors on them at five. Again Will seemed to take refuge in scholarly concentration. They covered more ground that day than Charlotte expected, especially with her brain straying back to memories of the night before. They were nearing the halfway mark in the book and her partner was driven. Charlotte, too, was increasingly invested in the stories and characters. Blustery Lepsch and wily Lady Satanay, Lady Tree, Pataraz and Nasra. Lady Sana, the forest mother, also known as Lovely Golden Knees. The names crowded Charlotte's subconscious along with her conflicted lust for Will.

Now, as they headed back to the cabin, she ached for him. Every night was like Chinese water torture, a drip drip drip of never-ending want. He probably felt the same, because a few minutes after they got back, he said, "Let's go to dinner in town. Let's get out of this wilderness and go to Maykop for the night."

Charlotte grimaced. "Is Maykop like Aleronsk?"

"Not at all. It's more 21st century. All the hotels have showers," he promised. "You'll be able to call your parents and catch up with your business partner."

Charlotte wasn't sure the hotel idea was prudent, but if it resulted in a shower… And calling home sounded wonderful. She packed an overnight bag, checking everything carefully for spiders beforehand. It took over an hour to get to their hotel on the outskirts of the capital. It wasn't five-star lodging by any means, but it was the most civilization Charlotte had experienced in weeks. Will reserved one room, representing them as a married couple.

"We don't have to have sex," he promised as they walked down the hall. "It's a safety thing." Charlotte didn't argue.

Will picked up the phone as soon as they got in the room, but the first order of business for Charlotte was a long hot shower. As she stepped into the soothing, misty spray, she knew she'd remember that shower the rest of her life. The pressure of the water, the lavender smell of the shampoo. Ecstasy.

Afterward, she brushed out her hair and dried it with the luxury of the wall-mounted hotel dryer, and slipped into one of the provided terrycloth robes feeling blissfully clean. By the time she was done, Will was off the phone, lounging on his bed. She didn't have to look at him to feel his eyes following her around.

She dialed her mother on the tabletop phone. What would she say to her? How to explain her adventures so far? She wanted to ask Will for privacy, but there was nowhere else to send him. After a few pointed glares, he shrugged and went in to shower. Both her mother and Roger wanted to know all about the Caucasus region and about her work, but it was hard to explain it to them with any justice.

As for the rest, she was close-lipped. The episode on the dirt road to Aleronsk would have terrified her mother, and Roger would never believe the shabby squalor of the cabin in which she lived. She completely glossed over the fact that Will was young and handsome, letting her mother go on believing he was an old man. Neither one seemed very interested in her disjointed retellings of the myths she was translating. They both assured her that everything back home was fine, saying in as many words that she wasn't missed at all.

Near the end of her conversation with Roger, Will exited the bathroom with his usual flagrant nudity. "God, that felt great," he yelled, knowing full well the person on the phone would hear it.

"Who's that?" Roger asked.

"My research partner. Dr. Mayfair." She made a face and gestured for him to get dressed. When he started doing the naked penis dance instead, she turned away, sucking her teeth.

"So, is he a good guy?" Roger asked.

Charlotte couldn't resist stealing a look at Will's ass as he leaned down to pull on a pair of cargos. "You would like him."

"Well, I'll let you go, boss. I don't want you to worry about a thing. Check in when you can."

"I definitely will. Bye. I miss you," she added impulsively before they hung up. It was a little depressing to hear the voices of her loved ones so far away.

"Ro-zhay, huh?" Will smirked as she placed the receiver back in the cradle. "You said you didn't have a boyfriend."

"I don't. He works for me. He's my assistant."

"That's your story, is it?"

"It's the truth." She could have told him Roger was gay, but she enjoyed the note of jealousy in Will's voice.

They walked to a restaurant across from the hotel. Perhaps in reaction to perceived competition, dinner was a never-ending stream of flirtatious banter. The scholar of hours before had disappeared, transformed into the Casanova again. She shut him down as well as she could, concentrating instead on the missed pleasure of fine dining. Will's cooking was good, but it was cabin cooking. This was restaurant cooking. If she tried hard, she could almost imagine herself at some place on the Riverfront, chatting with a group of her friends. God, she was homesick.

Afterward, Will asked for coffee, and Charlotte tried to avoid any thoughts about returning to the hotel room with him. The waitress was gone too soon, leaving them alone. The restaurant emptied. Will toyed with the sugar bowl, and she knew what was coming.

"Sweets for the sweet?" he asked, offering it to her.

"You know, for the rest of my life, whenever I see a spoonful of sugar, I'm going to think of you."

He smiled as he measured the exact amount she liked into her cup. "That's why I do it. I never want you to forget me."

What a ridiculous statement. How could she forget him? But when they parted, when this adventure was over, perhaps he would fade from her mind—eventually. In twenty, thirty years, would she still think about him and this time in the Caucasus? She stirred her coffee while Will stared down into his cup. His glance flicked across the room.

"She looks so much like you."

Charlotte didn't have to turn to know who he was talking about. She and the waitress shared a striking resemblance. The hair, the shape and color of their eyes.

"Easy to tell you're from this part of the world," he said.

Charlotte shrugged. "I doubt the bloodline's very pure anymore."

"You know what they used to call women from around here? Circassian beauties. They were renowned."

"I've never heard of that."

"Men used to come from all over the world to steal Circassian women. They were considered the most beautiful and elegant women in the world. Highly desirable as concubines."

She rolled her eyes. "You're so full of it sometimes."

"By the 1800s, there was an established sex trade here. Fathers sold their own daughters into slavery for an easy buck. *Sex* slavery."

"Very nice."

"Maybe your great-great-great-great-grandfather sold some hapless ancestor of yours into the hands of a perverse Persian prince."

"That sounds about right."

He took a sip of coffee, regarding her over the rim of his cup. "You don't believe me." He put it down and leaned forward, lowering his voice. "I can so easily see you in some palace, draped over a pile of velvet pillows. Everything melting and submissive, except for those eyes."

She couldn't look at him, couldn't dwell on the picture he drew in her mind. She didn't dare imagine him as the imperious prince, ordering her to her knees and bending her to his will. "You have a vivid fantasy life," she said in a tight voice.

"Do I? Maybe. I think you do too."

She stared at her lap, feeling his gaze rather than seeing it.

"Charlotte." His voice was like honey. "Want to play sultan and slave?"

* * * * *

There were no velvet pillows, no beaded curtains, no incense. No gold bangles or filmy veils, but he stripped her inside the utilitarian hotel room just like a greedy sultan, and like a newly acquired slave, Charlotte didn't resist. No, she kissed him as hungrily as she had the night before, let him seduce her without the least protest. He detached the leather strap from her bag to cinch her hands together. She clutched them now, as if in prayer, in front of her breasts as he tore off his clothes. He stared at her when he was nude—her golden, white-blond sultan. His cock stood up rigid, bowing forward. He watched her study it with a wicked curve to his lips. A tail dangled from the strap around her wrists. He used it to yank her to her knees.

"I hope you're worth your asking price." He said it in her grandfather's dialect. It momentarily befuddled her to hear the language on his lips.

"You will never subdue me," she replied in kind. She thought *subdue* might trip him up, but he seemed to figure it out by context. His cock reared up before her eyes, close enough to taste it.

His wicked smile lengthened. "I love a challenge. Service me, slave."

For slave, he used the word for servant, and she considered correcting him. *This is no time for language lessons!* Instead, she shook her head in reply to his command, caught up in the spirit of the role play.

His eyes widened. "You dare to deny me?" Her breath came faster beneath his piercing stare. He reached to the floor for his pants and drew out his weathered leather belt. *"Düşün mak yn?" Do you want to reconsider?*

Her hands shifted in their bonds as the stream of her arousal gushed into a sea. *Oh my God. What is going on here? And why am I playing along?* She lifted her chin. What would a Circassian woman do? She squared her shoulders and spat at him.

He laughed once, a wild, giddy laugh, and flew into motion. He pulled her up and off balance, throwing her onto the bed. She screamed, a real scream, and shied away as he shook the belt at her, falling over pillows and the balled-up comforter. "Don't hit me!"

He lunged at her and they knocked heads, laughing. "I won't hit you," Will said. "But cower some more. It turns me on."

"Please, Sir Sultan!" she wailed.

He stroked the belt down the outside of her thigh, then rose up and drew it right between her legs. The caress of the leather, the feigned threat in his expression aroused her more than she could have ever imagined. "Will you obey now?" he asked.

She shifted, staring at the hard, hot length of his shaft against her waist. She met his eyes with a shiver. "Yes. I will bend to your will."

He bared his teeth at her in an evil, lurid smile. "You are a very wise servant."

He misused the word again. She whispered, *"Kojl."* Slave.

He sucked in a breath and yanked her from the bed back to the floor. She waited on her knees, hunched over and feeling very much like a *kojl* as he went for a condom. She was so horny for Will, for her sultan, whatever he was. Her face burned with shame, but her clit ached for satisfaction. She whimpered as he prodded her into position with the belt, making her straighten her back and thrust her chest out. He pulled and pinched her nipples until she struggled away. "Do not be a naughty slave," he said. He used the right word this time. She stopped her writhing and let him hurt her. The harder he pinched, the more her pussy throbbed.

He gave her a haughty look. "It will please me to break your spirit." At that, he grasped the back of her neck and pressed the head of his cock to her lips. She opened for him, wanting to play the reluctant slave, but at the same time truly wanting to take him in her mouth. She'd never been a fan of blowjobs, but now... She would do anything for him at the moment. He was so hard, like steel. He moved his hips, holding her captured. His other hand grabbed the trailing strap, holding it taut so her fingers had nothing else to do but cup and fondle him. She caressed his balls and was rewarded with a growl and the feel of them drawing up tight. She could sense his tightly wound control in the rigid way he bucked between her lips. She used her tongue to tease his shaft, running it from the broad base up to the bulbous reddening peak.

He gave a hoarse groan and pulled away from her. He turned her around none too gently and bent her over the bed. He nudged her knees wide with his knees, squeezing and pinching her bottom cheeks, then snaked a hand beneath her to stroke her pussy. She moaned out loud at the aching heat it brought. She was so wet she was drowning. He pressed into her, driving all the way until he was balls deep. She felt conquered, invaded. She cried out and pitched her hips forward, but he pulled her back and plunged into her again.

They battled and fucked and struggled with one another while she climbed to an aching, bittersweet climax. She imagined she was really a Circassian love slave being bent to a sultan's will. He whispered threats and challenges against her ear in a guttural, dying language and she sobbed back in the same rare tongue.

When she came, she pounded the bed with her bound fists in violent frustration, finding herself enslaved yet again.

Will grasped her when he came to rest from the furor of his orgasm, only because he expected her to turn on him. He waited, dreading her scold, her anger, but she stayed still beneath him. He cradled her, overwhelmed by the intensity of their scene. He was still inside her, still joined to her. He never wanted to leave.

"Oh, Will," she sighed.

"Oh, Will, what?"

"I wonder."

He stared at her shoulder, thought about biting it. "You wonder what?"

"I wonder if I sold myself into sexual slavery when I came here."

"Oh, come on."

He eased out of her, taking care of the condom in the bathroom and returning to find her sprawled on the bed, a speculative look on her face.

"It's funny, how hard Ivo begged me to come here once he met me."

"Charlotte." He lay down beside her, bracing.

"And funny how I'm the only one, the only one out of all the people in the whole wide world who can read that dialect."

He smoothed back a lock of her sex-tousled hair. "What, do you think I sent Ivo out to pimp me the hottest translator available?"

"Yes."

"That I tried to send home as soon as she arrived?"

"That was obviously a psych-out."

"That speaks this extremely rare dialect?"

"You probably told him exactly what to find. Brown hair, hazel eyes."

"I prefer blondes." He ducked as her cinched fists flew toward his face. "Kidding! I was kidding. Why can't we bask in the afterglow like normal couples?"

She waved her hands in front of him, her lovely, sexy trapped hands. "Unbind me."

He grinned at her. "Why would I unbind my *kojl*?"

She gave him a look that promised mayhem and he decided not to press his luck. For once she wasn't running away or scolding him to stop seducing her. He took her hands and unwound the sloppy knot, setting the strap aside.

"Thank you," he said.

"For what?"

For giving me the best sex of my life. For not being angry afterward. "For this," he finally answered, pulling her right against him.

She felt so perfect in his arms. God, he was falling for her harder every day and he didn't know what to do about it.

"You're not angry this time?" he said against her neck.

"I want to be, but I'm not. I wanted this. I've tried not to want you, but I can't help myself."

"Thanks. I think."

She drew back and looked away from him. "I'm tired of resisting. I know it's going nowhere, but I don't care anymore."

He wanted to protest, to say they might go somewhere. He wanted to tell her love lies and all the romantic things she wanted to hear, but he wouldn't do that to her. His life hadn't been structured for long-term relationships in a long time. Even if he was willing to take a shot at a serious relationship, she wasn't going to leave behind her business and family back in the States.

No, her capitulation was a gift, a generous favor, and he would appreciate it as such. He would never take her for granted; he'd give her all the pleasure he could. He took her hand and kissed her palm. "You're wonderful, Charlotte."

That wasn't a lie. He could say it without the least bit of guilt.

Later, after they showered, they spread their notes on the bed and worked on the text. Will couldn't concentrate with her lying beside him. Her eyes were so lovely, her gaze so intent and intelligent. He watched her mouth the words, tapping her pencil. Even her tapping and jiggling didn't put him off anymore. She wrinkled her brow over a passage, running her fingers over it.

"What's wrong?" he asked quietly.

"I can't figure this out."

"Figure what out?" He bowed his head beside hers, transported by the soft tease of her hair.

"*Kay' shezch*," said Charlotte. "It must mean tears falling, but why would he cry here? He's a big tough warrior."

He scanned the section she was working on. "He's with a woman?"

"Yes."

"Tears equal semen."

"What?"

"In some mythologies, when men cry, they're actually... impregnating." He sifted through her notes, reading ahead. "A little further along, there'll be a baby."

"Oh yes, here." She pointed to a subsequent section. "She wraps up a rock in a blanket. Swaddles a rock? So the rock symbolizes a baby?"

"These devices are common across the mythologies of this region. Babies as rocks, tears as semen." He covered her tapping pencil with his hand and leered at her. "I'm starting to feel a little sad myself."

"Stop."

He leaned into her, breathing down her neck. "I might break out in tears. It's been so long since I had a good cry."

"It's been like, one hour," she said, nudging him away. "We have to finish this, don't we?" God, she smelled so good. What was she going on about? "So we can go home? There's going to be a war. Didn't you say that?"

"Yes, fine. I'll leave you alone." He refocused on his notes. "Back to work."

"Thank you."

He lasted all of two minutes before he tilted her chin up to kiss her. She was so lovely, so yielding and sweet. "Charlotte. I want you again. Please."

"Will."

"Please."

"You're incorrigible," she whispered against his lips.

He moaned. "I love when you use big words."

Her eyes fluttered at him as he insinuated a hand between her legs. "You're intractable, Will Mayfair. Irredeemable. Licentious. Profligate. You really are."

"Profligate? My God, woman. Have mercy." He pulled her under him, slipping his hands beneath her sleep shirt to caress her tautening nipples. She sucked in a breath and arched her body to his. Their notes slid under them, forgotten.

"Obstinate," she chided, before he silenced her with another kiss.

Chapter Nine: Complicated

After their stay at the Maykop hotel, life changed for Will. As the summer sun reached its zenith, they stayed indoors and burned up the sheets. He pleasured her, he flirted with her, he made her orgasm until she begged off in exhaustion. When it wasn't too hot, between work and sex, they walked to the lake and slid under the water together and looked up at the sun through the murky ripples.

It felt perfect to him. For the first time in his life, he had every kind of happiness. Success with Charlotte, success at work. A virtually extinct language coming back to life, and her gorgeous lips speaking it.

Charlotte was more excited about the stories than the language. She read to him now, sprawled on her back by the lake, sunbathing in bra and panties. She used her notes to block out the glare of sunshine while he lay beside her, drifting on the dulcet tones of her voice.

"On his travels, the warrior happened upon a magnificent copse of trees in dense forest. He said to himself, 'What is this place?' A woman answered him, saying, 'I am the Tree Goddess. This is my realm, and you are the first man to come here.'"

She glanced over at him, a twinkle in her eye. He smiled at her. "Go on."

She looked back at her notes. "Her hair reached up like branches to the skies, to learn all the wisdom of the heavens."

As she spoke, he pulled strands of her long hair and spread them over the ground like branches. He could see every color of nature in her hair. He could see her in every story she read.

"Her body was tall and fine, strong and unbending like a tree trunk." Yes, it was. "Her feet were like roots to the ground, so she never forgot that the earth gave all life."

She stopped reading as he leaned to kiss her. The sun felt hot on his bare back. He wanted to get naked, strip out of his shorts and take her on the ground. Her toes curled into the sand as he stroked a hand down her thigh.

"Her eyes were the most beautiful on earth," she said, shivering, "for they saw what other eyes could not." *Her lips were the most beautiful on earth, for they spoke what other lips could not.*

He was falling in love with her. He couldn't stop the slow, inevitable slide. He worked a finger beneath one side of her bra, but she put a hand over his, stopping him.

"You said you would listen."

"I am listening."

She gave him a skeptical look and rattled her papers as he moved his hand to the other breast.

"This wise and magnificent goddess welcomed the warrior into her realm. He pleased her so much she took him to her bed, and there he gave her great joy for seven days and seven nights."

"Lucky warrior."

She squirmed and half-closed her eyes at his leisurely sensual assault. "He..." She focused back on her notes with some difficulty. "He satisfied her so well that she glowed and fell in love with him. She told him, 'You are the first man to give me such pleasure.'"

She looked over at him with such open longing he was lost. Will fell on her, kissing, grasping. She laughed under the rash barrage of affection. "Quit, I'm not done." She pushed him away and rolled onto her stomach, her tanned calves weaving in the air.

"But when the seventh day came, he rose from her bed, still determined to find the edge of the earth. She begged him, 'Stay, and be my beloved! Do not continue on your quest.'" Charlotte stopped reading, her countenance darkening.

"Foolish warrior," Will said. "I would have stayed." He kissed the side of her neck, just below her earlobe. "I'd like to lay with you for seven days and seven nights. Make you glow." He smiled, but she frowned.

"Isn't that what you've been doing?" Charlotte asked. "And no, he doesn't stay. He leaves. You'll leave me too. You'll go back to London when we're finished."

He reoriented himself to the new direction of the conversation. "Maybe. Probably. That's where I live. I work there."

"I thought you worked here."

"I'm here on a grant, but I still have professional duties, papers I've got to publish. Classes to teach. Eventually, grant money runs out."

There was an awkward pause. Why should he feel guilty? He'd done nothing to lead her along. "Look, I don't think I've been dishonest with you. I'm not really— I'm not— With my work taking me so many places—"

"I know."

"I travel a lot. I work long hours."

"I know."

"We're just having fun here, right? And it's been fun."

She sat up, drawing away. "It's just, sometimes you look at me, like, just now...and I think maybe..."

"Maybe what?"

"Maybe you have feelings for me." Oh God, she put herself out there. So raw, so vulnerable. He took shelter in a grope and a laugh.

"Feelings? I have feelings for you, all right. Long, hard feelings."

She pushed him away and leaped to her feet, heading back toward the cabin. He was tempted to let her go, to let it end there, but he followed instead. She walked faster, jerking away when he tried to take her hand.

"You never listen to me, Will. I try to talk to you, but all you do is paw at me."

"God, the talk. The fucking talk. Why do women have to take everything, *everything*, and ruin it with words? Why?"

"What's wrong with words? Don't you speak, like, thirty languages? Aren't words your life?"

"It's my work. Words are work for me."

She spun on him, high color in her face. "Words are why I'm here, right? I'm trying to understand all this."

He flung his arms out in frustration. "Understand what, princess? You want words? *Relationship. Love. Future.* Will he take me to London? Will he come to America? Does he only want to sleep with me? Will he be my prince?"

She shook her head and turned her back on him, climbing the stairs to the porch as he carried on.

"Will he marry me? Does he love me, or is he just using me?"

"No." She spun on him again. "I already know you don't love me. I don't care. I don't care about our future."

"You say you don't, but you do. You want to hem up everything in nice clear little boxes so you can control your world, so you can arrange things the way you think they should go."

"No, I don't."

"You want to organize me."

"You know what I want?" she yelled, poking a finger in his chest. "I want a translation. Your language to mine. Because I don't understand right now what's going on between us."

He took her little poking finger and pushed it aside. His mouth assaulted hers as he crushed her against him. He couldn't give her words, but he would make things clear if that's what she wanted. She resisted at first, but he kissed her until she responded, until she pressed against the front of him taking little gasping breaths. "I'll translate for you," he said, lifting her so she could more easily wrap her legs around him. "Your room or mine?"

"No."

"Your room or mine?" he asked again.

"Yours has less spiders."

He carried her in and stripped her, and laid her on the bed. He pushed her back and spread her legs, then stood again. "Don't move a muscle. Not an inch." He ran out to the car, rummaging under the seats until he found the rope. When he returned, she was lying just as he'd left her. He shrugged out of his clothes and took up the four lengths he'd cut, wishing they were softer. They would have to do. He sat beside her and secured one wrist to the bedpost, then moved around to tie the other. "Translation:" he said. "You're not getting up until I say so."

He ran a finger down her thigh. Her leg jumped when he reached for her ankle. He tied it to the bottom bedpost. "Do you need a translation for this?" he asked as he tied the other one. She shook her head, a jerky movement. He knelt between her tied-open legs and ran a finger through glossy curls to her sodden center. She was breathing fast and shallow. When he found her clit, she came up off the bed. "Or is this kind of self-explanatory?" She bit her lip as he put a hand on the inside of each thigh, spreading her even wider.

"I... I'm pretty sure I understand."

"Let me explain a little more."

She hissed and arched her hips as he blazed a trail through the delicious heat of her pussy. *Lepsch set out to find the edge of the earth. He went in search of novel and interesting things.*

"Will!"

Her hands twisted in the bonds, in the scratchy ropes. "Be still," he said. "I don't want you to hurt yourself."

He kissed up the womanly curve of her hip to the bounty of her breasts. He suckled her, his cock feeling heavy and full as she moved under him as far as the ropes would allow. He licked up her chest to kiss her neck, her breathless lust noises resonating against his lips, then he spread her hair on the pillow as he'd spread it on the shore of the lake.

"Her hair reached to the skies, to learn all the wisdom of heaven," he said. It was so soft, so luscious. She sighed, her chest rising against his.

He knelt up, grabbing a condom from the side table. His gaze swept over her long legs, her flat stomach and the twin peaks of her perfect breasts. "Her body was tall and fine." She looked at him with those devastating Circassian eyes. If it had been him those many centuries ago, he would have purchased this beauty in a heartbeat. He would have secreted her away where no one could find her, and made love to her until the end of time.

He trailed a finger down her cheek, watching her eyelids flutter. "Her eyes were the most beautiful on earth, because they saw what others could not," he whispered. She stared at him, her eyes like liquid jade. He slid inside her, holding her gaze, enraptured. Her arms strained to break free, to hold him. Instead he held her close, his wet, willing captive. His Circassian beauty, captured and secured. He moved in her and out again, feeling every shiver and shudder, basking in the tension that racked her. "Charlotte..." *Don't you understand? There are no words for this.*

He made love to her until she trembled and embraced him in the only way she could. When he found his own release and pounded hard inside her, she didn't struggle against the ropes, only lay still and open to him, with her thick hair and cat eyes, and her body tall and fine.

Wise and magnificent goddess. Translation was so complicated sometimes.

* * * * *

By the time Will untied her, Charlotte was exhausted. She rested next to him in the darkening room. He held her back to his front, and she spooned inside the cave of his strong chest. As always, she weathered an inevitable plunge in mood. This was going to end far too soon for her liking. She already mourned what she'd lose.

"Are you falling asleep?" Will whispered.

"No, I'm awake."

He pulled her more tightly against him, oblivious to her mood, or not caring. "There's a language they used to speak in this part of the world, called Ubykh," he said. "It's extinct now. The last native speaker died a few years ago." He ran a fingertip across her arm, up and back. "It's a complicated language. It has eighty-one consonants, but only three vowels."

"Fascinating," Charlotte said.

"And it was never written down, not anywhere. Only spoken. It didn't have a written form."

"Wow, that's so interesting."

"Mm. Forget it."

She wished she didn't always feel so prickly after sex. It wreaked havoc on their pillow talk.

"You know, I listen *ad nauseum* to these stories you're translating," Will said, turning away from her in a huff.

"That I'm translating for you."

"But when I want to talk about something I find interesting—"

"All right. Fine. Eighty-one consonants."

"No, I'm not telling you now."

Charlotte stared at his back, at the myriad freckles there. "I promise I'll listen now. Please tell me."

"No, you've hurt my feelings." He rolled on his front, punching up his pillow. "You know, I don't talk about language with all the women I meet. Only the special ones."

"I'm one of the special ones?"

"I thought you were, but now I remember, you're just annoying."

"Forgive me," she said, rubbing his shoulder. "I'm listening now. U-bick?"

"Ubykh." He turned back to her. "What I was going to tell you is that in Ubykh, the words 'I love you' translate literally to 'I see you well.'"

Charlotte took his hand, pressed it against her cheek. "Oh, yeah?"

"Yeah. I always thought that was pretty cool." He slid his fingers down to cup her chin, then leaned to lick her neck in a slow arc.

"Maybe they were onto something," she sighed.

Will made a noise of agreement, drawing her hand down to rest on his hardening shaft. "My cock sees you well. That's for sure."

Charlotte laughed helplessly and covered her eyes. He pulled her hands away, not allowing her to hide. His touch smoothed over her skin, but she didn't feel it as much as the heat in his gaze. What was that heat, if not love?

"Let me see you." He said it like a caress.

She felt perilously close to crying. "Do you mean that in the Ubykh-ish sense?"

"I don't think 'Ubykh-ish' is a word, lovely girl."

"Can't we just make up the words we want?"

He brushed away the first tear as it fell. "It doesn't work that way." He shook his head at her. "That wouldn't be very organized, would it?"

Laughter, tears. It all blended together as he made love to her again. He was slow this time, deliberate. It wasn't the usual frenetic explosion, but a lazy meandering act accompanied by her sniffles and sighs. He licked away her tears with little remonstrances as he made her body ache with pleasure.

"Will," she gasped. "It feels too good. How do you do it?"

He pulled her onto her side, and then on top of him. "Do you want me to stop?"

She shook her head, bracing her hands on his chest, sliding up and down the length of his shaft. *I see you well.* She saw the strong curve of his shoulders. The intensity of his ice blue eyes. She studied the tension in his lips. He was Will, frustrating and wondrous, and she'd always love him. This was their time together, their precious time out of civilization, the past and present blended in their intense connection. The future was later...she'd worry about that later.

Her mind went blank as her climax approached and then unfurled, a well-tended fire stoked finally to awesome flame. She collapsed against his chest, practically speaking in tongues.

He dug fingers through her hair. "Oh, I liked that, Charlotte."

I loved it. I'll remember it all my life. She didn't say it out loud for fear of ruining the moment. Plus she was too sexed out to talk. They lay together, breathing in and out. She would remember everything about this, down to the gentle tickle of his breath against her skin. The ropes from earlier were still draped over the headboard, and their clothes strewn all over the floor.

It was not at all organized, but she wasn't going to fight it.

"Let me up, my Circassian siren," Will whispered. She shifted away so he could take off the condom. A moment later he gasped. "Jesus." He held up a busted, ragged piece of latex. "I think it broke."

He blinked at her, and she stared back. Uh, yeah. It was definitely broken.

"I'm not sure if it broke before or after," he said. "Can you...can you tell?"

They both leaped up and started combing over the sheets. Nothing. She ran into the bathroom and locked the door. She ran water and started washing herself, knowing with the reasonable part of her brain that it would accomplish nothing at this point. The unreasonable part of her brain still had to wash. She put her head in her hands when he knocked.

"No. Go away."

Silence, and then another knock. "Let me in."

She wrapped a towel around herself and unlocked the door. He opened it, looking considerably paler than usual.

"I'm sorry. I didn't know it had broken."

"Yeah, well, you being sorry doesn't help me."

The words sounded too harsh, especially after the connection that had come earlier. She wanted to take them back but he'd already heard them. Some softness in his face fell shuttered. "I'm clean, you know. If that's what you're worried about."

She rubbed her forehead. "That's so not what I'm worried about."

He swallowed hard. "Where are you in your cycle?"

"My cycles are irregular. I don't know. Maybe that means it's less likely that...something will happen."

Will clasped his hands in front of his mouth and bowed his head, thinking. "Okay, we can go into Maykop. We'll go tomorrow. They've got to have something there. Morning-after pills or something." He looked back up at her. "Everything will be okay. I'll take care of things, no matter what. I promise."

You're a liar, she thought. *I don't trust you and I don't believe you.*

And I hate that all of this feels so dangerous and uncontrolled and that I love you anyway.

Chapter Ten: Panic

In Maykop, the first two doctors they visited refused to help because they were foreign and unmarried. They posed as a married couple at the third doctor's office, but he claimed to have no access to a morning-after contraceptive. He offered condoms and birth control pills when Charlotte started crying. Will pocketed them, desperate for anything at that point. At the hospital, they were turned away because of their foreign passports, and directed back to the same private doctors who'd already failed to help.

Now they sat in the car, defeated. Every time she sniffled beside him, Will's heart clenched. This was his fault. She'd told him to leave her alone, but he hadn't listened. This was the absolute worst place in the world to have a screw up like this. He wished he could go back in time and keep his dick in his trousers, but she'd made it impossible. Even now he wanted to kiss and caress her, even now in her misery. He wanted to make all her fears go away, but he didn't know how.

"Maybe we should go to Tbilisi," he said. "It's a bigger city."

"How far is that?"

"Nine or ten hours. But that's the biggest city around here, and probably our best chance."

"What if we drive all that way and get the same runaround?"

"What else is there to do?"

She picked up the bundle of contraceptives, turning the pill packs over in her hand. "Maybe if I take a whole bunch of these... It'll screw up my hormones, right? I read somewhere that the morning-after pill is just a huge dose of the same hormones in birth control pills."

He snatched them back. "That could make you really sick. Let's not try to wing this one. The real morning-after pill is bad enough." He didn't want to say it, but he had to. "You need to go home. You could fly out of Krasnodar tomorrow morning. You could be at a clinic in the States by the afternoon."

She bit her lip. He hated that she was even considering it, but he also knew he should urge her to go.

"What about the text?" she asked. "We're not finished yet."

He dug deep and forced the words out. "I've got enough. And you could always come back." He knew she wouldn't come back. *Don't go. Don't leave me. Bloody hell. It's too soon.*

She was quiet a long time, blowing her nose and rubbing at her eyes. "You know what? I think we're overreacting. I doubt I can even get pregnant. My cycle is so crazy and it was only that one time. I don't want to fly all the way home on some teeny, tiny chance I might be pregnant and find out it was all for nothing."

"Are you sure?" Will held his breath. He would drive her right to the airport if she wanted it, if she asked. She bit a finger and thought for a moment.

"If worse comes to worse, if I have to make some decisions later, I will. But the chance is so small. I don't want to worry about it anymore. I sure as heck don't want to fly over the mountains in a prop plane the way I'm feeling right now."

Will laughed, a deep exhale of relief. "You know, I've never made anyone pregnant, and there have been accidents. All false alarms. Maybe we are overreacting a bit."

"Yeah. There's something about being in a foreign country that makes emergencies seem much more...scary. Some added desperation when you aren't close to home."

He took her hand, watching the passersby in the street. He knew about desperation in a foreign country. He'd been devastated for her in the doctor's office when she'd broken down in tears. She didn't even speak the local language. She was making so many sacrifices for him. For words. For the words of a culture that wasn't even around anymore.

A couple of men walked by, talking animatedly. Through the buffer of the windows he caught words that unnerved him, words about war and preparation. The feel in Maykop was heightened, ratcheting up. The August heat seemed to stretch beyond weather to the people. He'd read the day's papers waiting in the doctors' offices, eavesdropped on conversations. There was nothing concrete to alarm him. Just a growing feeling...

He looked back at Charlotte, so vulnerable in this place. "Either way, we'd better finish as soon as possible. Maybe we should just copy the rest, and do the transcription somewhere safer." Ugh, wrong choice of words.

Her eyes searched his. "The war?"

"It's not imminent, I don't think, but I don't want to stay here a second longer than we have to. I don't want to press our luck."

"How will we know when it starts, way out by Aleronsk? Will the fighting even come out that way?"

"Eventually it will, for the mine and the oil fields. How long do you think it will take us to copy the rest of the text?"

"I don't know. A week or two?"

"I'll help. I'm not as fluent as you. I might get some wrong." He looked over at her, drank in all the loveliness of her, even with her red, swollen eyes. "I thought we would have more time. I wish we had more time." *I wish I could stay here with you forever, just you and me and the lake and the mountains, and you moaning against my ear.*

Charlotte nodded. "We should go back to Aleronsk right now and go back to work. The sooner we finish, the better."

"Do you want to call home first? While we're here in town?"

"No, not the way I feel now. Let's just get back to work so we can get out of this place."

It was like pulling his limbs through quicksand, to move toward an ending with her. "Yeah, okay. Sounds good."

* * * * *

They toiled over the little table in the back room every day, from the time the museum opened until the moment it closed. Charlotte copied the text word-for-word into notebooks and tried not to think about any of the other things on her mind. Whether her period would be late. Whether their little cabin would be bombed in the middle of the night. Whether she would ever see Will again once they hightailed it out of there.

Of course she would see him again, she told herself. There would still be work to do, the translation to finish. He'd talked about journal articles and even a book. She could get a direct flight to London any time of day out of Atlanta. *Yeah, Charlotte. He'll only be eight or nine hours—an entire ocean—away.*

But that was the future. This was the last bit of now, with his knee pressed against hers and his elbow just a few inches to the right. God, she would miss him so badly. She'd pushed him away for so long, believing they weren't compatible, would never be compatible. But now she wasn't so sure. They only had days left together to figure it out. Maybe a couple weeks. Sure, she could go to London with him to do the rest of the translations, but what about her business?

They'd end up working together online, most likely. It would be more practical, and easy enough to do when they got out of this wilderness and had a high speed Internet connection again. He'd go back to his teaching and researching, and she'd go back to organizing homes and arranging everything perfectly. Making everything calm and orderly. Taking showers and not worrying about big hairy spiders and her personal safety. It would be a good thing.

So why did she want to dawdle? Charlotte couldn't focus on the words. She'd reread a sentence and read it again, and Will wouldn't hurry her. But they *had* to hurry. War was scary, that was all she knew about it. She'd seen war on the news, seen it in books and magazines. Fighting was ugly and dangerous and she had no desire to be anywhere close to it, even with a U.S. passport in her hands. The nearest embassy was hours away in Tbilisi. Will kept the car full of gas, topping it off every day or two, which underlined for her how precipitous their position was.

Still, on the page, Lady Satanay continued her antics. The gods and goddesses frolicked and Lepsch slogged through his quest to the edge of the earth. Charlotte read along with jaded interest, knowing there was no edge. When would he realize it? Will, on the other hand, was over the stories, and completely absorbed in the language. She'd hear him muttering it under his breath, consigning words to memory or working out the complicated cases. At night, they ate ravenously, having skipped lunch, and worked on the translations as long as they could in the muggy summer air. They swam. They talked sometimes and joked together, but not as much.

He didn't touch her. Not once.

Charlotte knew it was for the best. She knew guilt weighed as heavily on him as fear weighed on her. What if she didn't get her period? That wasn't unusual for her. She wouldn't know for sure until she got home and took a pregnancy test. Then, of course, if she was pregnant she could take care of it. The thought of that made something twist in her heart. No, no... She wouldn't be able to get rid of it like some nuisance, not if it was his.

God, these thoughts.

The next day she hunched over the text, copying a passage that had her stumped. She kept hoping for a wrap up, a resolution, but the story was off on another tangent. She reread again, and then again, disequilibrated by the lack of understanding. *Just copy it, Charlotte. Figure it out later.* She set out to do that when the room vibrated with a low thump.

Will looked at her. "Did you hear that?"

Then they both heard it, a low rumble. In the eerie silence that followed, another thump vibrated the room. Will moved fast, with a focus that terrified her. "Get your notebooks. Everything. We're going to Krasnodar."

Charlotte's heart pounded. "What if that's where the sounds are coming from?"

Will ignored her, stalking around the room until he found a book the same size as the box that held the text. He thrust it inside and shut it, then slid the priceless artifact down into his laptop bag.

"Will!" Charlotte was horrified.

"He hasn't checked the box in weeks. We'll hand it over and he'll put it away like always. He'll never know."

"They'll find out eventually."

He zipped up his bag as another rumble sounded. "What use is this book to anyone but you, Charlotte?"

"I don't want to get in trouble."

"I'll keep it with me. If they catch me I'll tell them I was trying to keep it safe. And I will. I'll give it back when things settle down around here. This museum could be a pile of rubble in a week."

Charlotte gathered up her notes with trembling fingers. "Don't look guilty when we go out there," Will warned. "Don't look nervous."

It wasn't in Charlotte's power to look anything but terrified. The museum clerk met them at the door to the research room. He and Will exchanged a few hurried words, undoubtedly about the sounds outside. To her relief, the man carried the box away and stowed it without so much as a glance. Any glee she might have felt in getting away with their antiquity heist was drowned out by anxiety about their safety. *Maybe they're knocking down trees*, Charlotte thought. *Maybe some gas lines exploded. Maybe it's nothing.*

As soon as they stepped on the street, it became obvious it wasn't nothing. People were running around, gathering in clusters, pointing toward the east.

"Come on." Will touched her arm. "We need to hurry. We'll swing by the cabin to grab our things and head right back out."

It was quiet until they were almost to the site, and then the thumping started again. Long, sustained thumping that shook the entire car. The mountains were like echo chambers, the air as clear and still as a grave. As they parked, the rat-a-tat sound of distant gunfire had her running to her room. She grabbed a few things. A couple outfits, all her notebooks, stuffing them into her luggage. Will appeared at the door.

"Forget it. Bring what you have. Now."

"You're scaring me."

"Just do it." He came in and grabbed her bag. "We have to cross into Krasnodar Krai and figure out who's bombing who right now. We can come back another time for the rest. Do you have your passport?"

"Yes."

"Where?"

Charlotte dug in her purse and held it up for him.

"Don't let it out of your hands, no matter what." He shouldered her bag and ran out to the car to throw it in the back with his bag and laptop. It chilled her that he looked around the clearing before he would let her come out. The lights were still on in the cabin. Their coffee cups were still sitting on the table.

"Will—"

"Let's just go, Charlotte. I don't know what the roads will be like, or which airports will be open. I don't want to take fifteen minutes, I want to go now."

She felt hot all over, panic lodging in her throat as she got in and buckled her seat belt. "Are we going to be okay?"

"Yeah, don't worry. Just—"

Another boom, a louder one. It could have been a mile away or fifty miles away. The air lit up like heat lightning on a humid Savannah night.

"Are those bombs? What direction is that sound coming from?"

"I don't know."

"What if they're bombing Maykop? Or Krasnodar? They'll bomb the airports first—"

"Charlotte, I don't know!"

They took the turn onto the main road into Aleronsk, passing dark shacks along the street. "What if we can't get out? What will we do?" she asked.

"We'll figure it out."

"I don't want to die here!"

He held up a hand to silence her. "Please stop freaking out. Let's take it one minute at a time, okay? If we can't fly out, we'll go to the American embassy or the British embassy. Our passports will protect us."

"How? How will they protect us?" Ivo and Will both seemed to put a lot of stock in the saving power of a passport, but Charlotte was skeptical that a small paper booklet could keep her safe if a bomb dropped on her head. She started bawling and hated herself for it, but the hysteria was pouring out of her and she didn't know how to stop it. Will slowed the car and turned to her, taking her hand. He brought her fingers to his lips.

"Take some deep breaths, would you? Breathe for me."

"Where is everyone else?" Charlotte sobbed. "Why are we the only ones on the road?"

"Because we're the only ones with somewhere else to go. Now, calm down." He brushed back her hair and wiped away her tears. "It's too soon to panic. We could be overreacting again. Maybe this is nothing. Exercises. Warning shots." He put the car back in gear and started down the road. "Let's just be safe. Let's get closer to the airport and closer to a reliable news source."

It grew quiet again, no more booms, and Charlotte calmed a little. Exercises, of course. If there was going to be a war, troops would be running exercises. Just because they hadn't heard them before didn't mean they couldn't start them up now. But why this late in the day?

Will braked and Charlotte saw some kind of checkpoint set up ahead, with a handful of military vehicles. She reached for her passport in her bag to reassure herself it was there. Will took her hand and gave it a squeeze, forcing a smile she knew must have taken a great deal of effort.

"Maybe these guys will know what's going on. Sit tight. I'll see what I can find out."

She looked around at the armored vehicles beside the road, at the soldiers leaning beside them. Some were smoking, most were just standing around. One of them approached, peering inside the car as Will rolled down the window. He spoke to him in Adyghe, and the soldier responded in an affirmative tone. The look Will gave her said it all—something serious was going on. Will patted her hands where she wrung them in her lap, and spoke again to the soldier. From his gestures, Charlotte guessed he was explaining they were on their way out to Krasnodar Krai. At that point, the soldier switched to heavily accented English, leaning down to look at her.

"Pashkovsky Airport is closed." His dire inflection and the way he looked at her had her clutching her passport again.

Will spoke a little louder than usual, a little slower. "I'm a British citizen, and she's an American. We'll head to Tbilisi then, to the embassy."

"Which embassy?"

Will looked over at her briefly. "The American one, I suppose." A couple other soldiers approached, with a little too much interest for Charlotte's peace of mind. She couldn't have said a word to save her life. The soldier's gaze darted around the inside of the car, and then he opened Will's door with a muted click that stopped her heart. She thought of the stolen artifact in Will's bag and pushed down suffocating alarm.

"Is there some problem?" Will asked. "We'd like to get on—"

"What is your business here in Adygea?" interrupted one of the soldiers who'd come over. His English was stilted but his accusatory tone was impossible to miss.

Will's voice was respectful but firm. "We were working on a research project in Aleronsk. It's a MacArthur funded language project.

I've got paperwork in the back if you'd like to see it." The three soldiers stepped away to confer about this.

Charlotte glanced to her right and gasped. A man stared at her through her window. She knew him. He was one of the men who'd cornered her on the path by the miners' ghetto.

"What's going on?" she whispered. "Can't you just go?"

"No, I can't go. There are twenty armed guys out there. Stay calm. If you freak out, they'll freak out. Just sit there."

The first soldier returned to Will's side of the car. "You have passports?"

They both dug them out. Will handed them to the soldiers. The one she recognized, the one looking in from her side of the car, walked around to confer with them now. A moment later they were back again.

"He says you tell him she is your wife, and yet this passport is United Kingdom, and her passport is United States."

Will paled. He recognized him now also. "I did tell him she was my wife."

"This was a lie?"

Will's lips tightened. "Yes. But I had my reasons. I wanted him to leave her alone."

"She looks like Russian woman, not American." The soldier scowled at her and said something in Adyghe.

"She's not from here," Will insisted. "She's from the U.S. She works for me as a translator." He repeated the same thing in Adyghe. With a jolt, Charlotte realized she couldn't see her passport anymore.

"Will, what's going on?"

He held up a hand and she bit her lip. The hand he held up was shaking, and it scared her more than anything had ever scared her in her life. Will was *afraid.* Her stomach clenched and flipped over as more soldiers approached. They all consulted, and several looked in at her. Their light, exotic eyes held no reassurance. Any relief she felt to see her passport in the lead soldier's hand was erased by his next statement.

"This passport, I think it is not legitimate. This woman is perhaps Russian spy. She watches the mine."

Her door opened with a jarring click. "Will," she gasped. She struggled against the disembodied hand that reached for her.

Will's voice finally started to betray panic. "She's not a spy. She's a translator. She works for me."

The man with her passport frowned. "I think we take for questioning. To be safe."

The soldier on her side was reaching across her now, unbuckling her seat belt. "Will. Oh, God." Her voice came out a whisper, not the scream that threatened to break loose. They hauled her around to the other side of the car. Charlotte stared at her white-faced partner. He would work things out. He would fix this before it went any further. He said he wouldn't let anything happen to her.

"She's an American," Will insisted. "She's a fucking home organizer from Savannah, Georgia. She doesn't even speak Russian."

"You said she is your translator," said the soldier.

"She speaks Adyghe, not Russian."

"Ah, but I speak to her in Adyghe a moment ago and she pretends to misunderstand."

"No, she speaks a very old dialect. Look, I can explain. I can show you the work we've done. Let me show you."

He reached toward the back seat and twenty weapons were lifted in a sickening show of force. "Will!" Charlotte shrieked, but the sound of the guns being cocked had already stopped him. He froze and turned slowly, hands up. "Listen," he said to the lead soldier in a very quiet voice. "Just go with us to the embassy in Tbilisi. We'll straighten all this out." Will looked at her, just a fleeting moment. She couldn't read his face.

The soldier stopped him when Will moved to get out of the car. "Tbilisi is too far. Roads are not safe. There is a war on, you know." He handed back Will's passport and pocketed Charlotte's. "We question her, this is all. If she is really American, we let her go."

She recognized Will's expression finally. Helplessness. She understood, with sickening clarity, that he couldn't help her at all. His mouth worked but nothing came out for a few moments. "This—this is insane. Where are you taking her to question her? Who's in charge here?"

The more questions he asked, the more she understood her peril. They began to lead her away. She heard the head soldier dismissing Will with a few curt words in heavily accented English. "In these times, we cannot be careful enough. It is best if you go. You leave now."

Will protested in Adyghe. She didn't know what he said, didn't hear anymore except the crunch of the soldiers' footsteps as they led her across the clearing to one of the armored jeeps. They shoved her in the back. It smelled terribly of body odor and something else. Warfare. Weapons. She looked out the window at Will, still arguing with the head soldier.

Go, just go. They had their guns out. She was afraid for him. As long as she was afraid for him, she wouldn't have to think about her own situation. She wanted him to go before they shot him. Still, when he slammed the door and drove off, her eyes blurred and her stomach nearly emptied. She whimpered, alone behind grime-clouded windows, with the soldiers milling around outside.

She thought again of that thin hairline plane, the delineation between man and animal. Five men got into the car with her, two of them crowding her into the middle of the back seat. They didn't restrain her in any way, or even speak to her. They didn't have to. She had no power. They had it all.

Chapter Eleven: The Edge

They took her to someone's house. It wasn't a prison or any official building. She knew because there was a table against the wall with newspapers on it and dishes piled in the kitchen sink. They pretended to interrogate her while she alternated between crying and threatening them. She insisted they return her passport, demanded to be taken to the embassy in Tbilisi. She offered money and then threatened them with her father's lawyers. They yelled back at her, things she didn't understand.

Finally, the tall one, the one she remembered from the woods, advanced on her and shoved her to the floor. It was a shot across the bow. Their eyes locked, and Charlotte saw what was coming next. She felt horror but a sense of confusion too. What the hell was she supposed to do? How could she stop this? *Why was she here?*

He put a hand around her neck and tightened it, more, then a little more, still yelling in a garble of foreign syllables. When he put his hands under her clothes, grasping down her shorts and under her shirt, she started to fight. She'd never known if she'd be a fighter in this situation—but she was a fighter. He was disgusting, evil, and this was all unfair. She thought if she fought long enough, Will would come back with someone official to help her. She held onto that hope for a long time, or maybe only a few minutes, until the soldier choked her so hard that the world blurred.

They never even took her shirt off, just her shorts and her panties. She stared in a daze at the garments crumpled beside her waist. The first soldier shoved her thighs open and wrenched into her, shocking, jagged pain. She knew he was pretending to do it as some form of retribution, as part of the interrogation, to make her "talk." But she knew he really did it because he was a monster and a rapist and just felt like raping someone, so she still fought, even though she knew she was making things harder for herself. She fought not only because his violent thrusts were hurting her, but because she wanted them to know she saw through their act. They knew she wasn't a spy, like she knew they weren't real soldiers, just barbaric opportunists with uniforms and guns. When the first soldier finished, one of the others knelt on her chest and stayed there until three other men had raped her. Maybe he raped her too at the end. She couldn't remember. Her body froze, went numb, stopped feeling after a while. Everything got fuzzy. She couldn't breathe, she couldn't think.

Then the door banged open and her eyes focused warily on another pair of boots. She heard sharp words in Russian. Dust motes skidded across the floor, the men leaped away from her so fast. The new arrival was older, with more insignia on his uniform, and short hair of salt and pepper gray. He was tall, thin, with deep set eyes and a tanned, creased face. He was clean shaven rather than scruffy and unkempt like the others. His eyes communicated sympathy, and she realized he was here to help her, not to rape her next. She scuttled up and wrapped her hands around her legs, gazing into the eyes of her savior. She would always remember that particular shade of blue and the look on his face at that moment. The outrage, the regret.

Will wasn't with him, but that was okay. She was going to be okay now. She pulled on her shorts, not even bothering with her panties in her hurry. She balled them up and shoved them in her pocket instead, not willing to leave one part of her behind in this chamber of hell. She was

leaving part of herself behind though—the invulnerable part. The part that believed something like this could never happen to her. *This isn't a joke, Charlotte. I'm afraid you'll find that out as soon as you get there.*
Oh mama. You just don't know.

She sat beside the silent soldier in another army vehicle, trembling, hurting. God, now she hurt. She felt abraded, sore. Every time she shifted she felt wetness inside her and her gorge rose. She didn't know how she was going to go back and face her parents and her old life. And Will... *Will, you won't believe what they did to me.* She should have gone home when he told her to. She was the one who'd decided to stay here over and over again.

She thought maybe she wouldn't tell anyone. Maybe she would say they'd only interrogated her. Maybe she'd wake up and find everything was a dream. Maybe she'd wake up in the cozy, safe cabin and Will would be snoring beside her, muttering from time to time in some unknown language. Yes, she'd pretend it was all a dream and hadn't really happened. Just put it away like she put away her clients' clutter and mess.

But the man with her would have to make some kind of report about what happened. He'd arrived in the middle of things and seemed to be a high-ranking officer, if the men's deference to him meant anything. The soldiers would all be court-martialed. She might have to testify before some foreign military court. Oh God, she just wanted to scrub herself clean in an hours-long shower and go home.

From time to time the man looked over as if to judge her mental soundness, or the state of her health. She thought she should say something, thank him at least. She knew the words for "Thank you" but couldn't even bring herself to say that.

After about fifteen minutes they pulled off the main road and headed west. The vibrations still shook the ground but the sound was muted. She'd escaped. Maybe he was taking her to Krasnodar. Will would probably be there waiting for word of her. Will would make everything better. He would hug her while she cried, hold her until she collected her sanity, but she wouldn't tell him what they'd done to her. It wasn't his fault, and she didn't want him living with the guilt the rest of his life. She didn't want anyone to know about it, actually. That would be easiest for her. She'd insist that the soldier guy drop the matter, and she'd find a way to live with the secret for the rest of her life. He probably spoke enough English to understand her wishes.

She was about to turn to him with her request when they left the road and headed down a forested path. The wide vehicle clipped branches and bobbed through uneven holes in the terrain, so Charlotte was tossed around on her seat. He finally pulled into a dark clearing and cut the engine. He left the headlights on, trained on a ramshackle cabin even smaller than the one she and Will had shared.

No. Oh no.

The headlights clicked off, and so did Charlotte's false sense of safety. He wasn't her savior at all. He was going to kill her. She'd arrived at the place she was going to die. It would be too big a mess, a rich American girl assaulted by local soldiers. He was going to make a problem disappear, bury her somewhere in this clearing so she was never found, so his soldiers could continue to fight. She started to scream, she started to cry, started to plead and bargain and threaten, but it came out in panicked shrieks that probably made no sense to him.

He placed a finger on her lips. "Shh," he said. "Everything o-kay."

Relief choked her. Disbelief followed. Of course you'd say that to a hysterical, screaming woman you intended to knock off. She tried to open her door to run, but she was locked in. He jerked her out his side, pulling her behind him to the small cabin. She struggled with him all the way to the door, fell and scraped her knee. She thought, what does it matter? He's going to kill me. She'd take rape any day over this. Back in that house there had been a chance of rescue. She knew in this house there was none. He opened the door with a key and then kicked it shut behind them and flicked on a weak overhead light. There was a narrow bed, a sink and toilet, a shower with a drain in the floor, and dissonant floral curtains on the walls framing boarded-up windows. *Marimekko?* she thought wildly.

He hauled her to stand beneath the showerhead, stripped her, then turned on the water full blast, holding her under the lukewarm spray. Twice she tried to pull away from him and twice he slapped her so hard her eyes blurred. She was afraid he would break her teeth, and that would be the final straw, so she gave up then. Just for a while. She stood under the water and sobbed and let him wash the dirt and disgusting fluids away. Her stomach emptied. This too went down the drain while he made soft, sympathetic noises.

Would he kill her now? Weird, to clean up someone you planned to murder. He turned off the water and toweled her dry, then pushed her toward the bed. He undid his belt, his zipper. *No, not again.* She ran, only to be caught with a chuckle and flung back on the bed. He came over her, holding her down, pressing into her with rough jerks. It hurt like jagged glass. The numbness from before was gone and she felt every terrible stroke. He said gentle words she didn't understand while she thought about pain, about dying in terrible circumstances. This was how she would spend her last moments. Wild, disparate thoughts crowded her mind. Her parents' faces, Roger's teasing smile, her grandfather's laughter. Her ruffled bedcover and soft bed at home. Lepsch, the mighty warrior. Will. She pictured Will as she'd seen him when she got off the plane in Maykop. *Are you Charlie Rowe, by any chance?*

When the soldier finished and pulled away from her, she fell apart, awaiting death, but he kissed her forehead and then pressed his lips to hers, jabbing his tongue inside. It was thick and sour. She retched but there was nothing to come up. "No, no," he said. "Calm now."

She could barely catch her breath, she was crying so hard. He grabbed her by the arm and sat her naked on a wooden chair. He used black duct tape to bind her to it, her wrists, her ankles, her waist. Her choking hysteria subsided. Death wasn't imminent. He was restraining her. Leaving her. He said something to her, made the sign for food, bringing fingers to his mouth and pretending to chew. "Tomorrow," he said. "I come back. I bring food."

Charlotte stared, befuddled, as he left with her clothes, turning the light off behind him. In the complete black darkness, she heard a key scrape in a lock and then she screamed, only once. She didn't want him to come back and put tape over her mouth too. Instead she sat and made small squeaking sounds of panic. She tried to pry her hands and legs loose but only succeeded in knocking over the chair. She banged her head hard on the floor, breathed in a mouthful of dust and went still. Her limbs already ached.

The separating plane of madness and civilization, the thin delineation, was shattering beneath her, disappearing. She had nothing to float on, nothing to grasp. She'd found the edge of the earth. It was here, in the dark, where she smothered under a blanket of helplessness and terror. She'd found the edge of the earth, and she'd fallen off.

* * * * *

He came back the next day just as daylight started to fade from the crack beneath the door. She watched the crack all day, sleeping a little, crying a little, but mostly staring at that sliver of light in a daze. At one point, a big spider like the ones from their cabin made a slow, meandering jaunt across the floor to disappear beneath a knot in the wood of the far wall. She didn't move, even when it came within a few feet of her. Those spiders weren't the scariest things in her world anymore.

The scariest thing in her world was the tall, mild-eyed soldier who'd brought her here and taped her to this chair. How would anyone know where to find her? He certainly wouldn't tell them. *Men used to come from all over the world to steal Circassian women.* Will had warned her. So many warnings, all of them ignored.

Her jailer clucked over her when he found her on the floor lying in a puddle of urine. She'd held it as long as she could. She couldn't feel her arms or her feet.

He chafed her limbs until sensation returned, ignoring her alternate threats and tears. Another shower. Another gentle, solicitous raping on the creaking bed while she begged him to let her go. He shook his head and chided her afterward with new sharpness in his voice. It occurred to

Charlotte that her survival depended on his goodwill toward her. Somehow she read in that angry scold that he would dispose of her when he no longer needed or wanted her. He was a soldier. There was a gun sitting in the corner. He could kill her without blinking an eye and sling her body out into the deep forest to decompose. No one would ever know. Her parents and Will would have no sense of closure.

Will... It had been twenty-four hours now. They had to be looking for her. The soldiers might talk, might admit this man had taken her from their custody. Maybe this property was linked to his name, and police would storm in here any moment and free her.

But no, that didn't happen. Before the man left, he installed a system of cuffs and chains so she could at least use the bathroom and walk around. After he was gone, she yanked at the attachment bolt until her whole body ached and her wrists bled, but she couldn't get loose. She dragged her chains around like a ghost and slept because it was her only form of escape. A week passed. Two weeks. He fed her and bathed her, and raped her every visit, usually more than once. He made her suck him off, and she complied because he hurt her if she didn't. His cock gagged her and made her vomit.

Sometimes he skipped a day and she waited, starving, nauseous, panicked. She'd hear artillery and bombs and imagine the ceiling falling in on her. She'd imagine another group of soldiers finding her and assaulting her. She'd find herself in the sick situation of wanting him to come. At least when he was there she wasn't alone, abandoned. In the beginning, she'd imagined him killing her violently, with gunfire, but he could just as easily stop coming and let her slowly starve to death. No muss, no fuss, no blood to clean up afterward. She'd cry when she thought about things like that. She cried all the time. She began to hate her parents because they obviously weren't trying hard enough to find her. She hated Will with a bitter and aching heart. She hated Ivo for meeting her at the International Center. She hated the stories she'd translated, the stories that ran haphazardly through her head.

Two months went by, then three. She counted each day, imprinted each number in her head so she wouldn't lose track of time. Her body grew thin and weak even though he brought her healthful food, meat and cheese, fruit and vegetables. He brought piles of blankets as the weather grew colder, but she never stopped shivering. She was tired, deathly tired, and she knew he was getting bored with her.

She begged him to let her go home, making up wild stories of how she'd help hide what he'd done. Anything, anything to get away from him. He would stare at her, as if considering what to do with her. At the beginning he'd talked to her now and again, but now he said almost nothing at all. He began to rape her more roughly, without emotion. Every time now, afterward, she expected him to put a pillow over her face, or go for his gun. Every time he left she watched him go with wide eyes, afraid he wasn't coming back. She'd lie in the dark, heedless of spiders, almost wanting to die to get it over with.

Then she felt it. A movement she thought was hunger, a flutter below her waist. She ignored it, but then she felt it more and more, often right after she'd eaten. It occurred to her that it was too consistent, and somehow too deliberate, to be hunger pangs.

She realized there was a baby growing inside her. She'd assumed her lack of periods was due to stress, her nausea and exhaustion from the trauma of her captivity. This new development panicked her. Once he found out, she was pretty sure it would mean the end of her life. Or would it? Would he let her go if he knew she was pregnant? The reality of the being inside her hardly registered. It was the consequences she obsessed about. The fallout—because she could only hide a pregnancy for so long.

In the end it didn't matter, because he stopped coming. Two days, three days. Four days. She had water, but no food. She chewed at her nails, ravenous, shivering. She wondered how long she would last before she went after the spiders, choking them down for their meager nutritional value. She wondered how long death by starvation would take. She felt the baby moving inside her and felt terribly sad for both of them. Not one death, but two. She put her hands over her stomach, over the tiniest bump of her womb, and felt pity for her baby of indeterminate paternity. She pretended it was Will's, because it brought her comfort to have some part of him with her.

She selfishly hoped she would die first, because she didn't want to die alone.

Then, on the eighth day she heard a car engine in the clearing—and it wasn't his. She knew the sound of his, could pick it out a mile away, she listened for it so closely. She started to scream. Enemy or friend, she didn't care. She needed food. She needed human contact. Her baby needed help. She screamed until she tasted blood in her throat while a male and female voice called from outside. She didn't know what they said, didn't remember the door opening.

Charlotte woke up in a white, sterile hospital room with an IV in her arm. It turned out her jailer, a decorated military commander named Rado Damir, had been killed in a skirmish the week before. His daughter and her husband found out about the cabin while going through his papers. They were having financial difficulties, and had hoped to uncover some money. If they hadn't needed the money, if they'd waited to settle his estate, it would have been too late for her.

Her mother and father flew over and gave the couple a big reward, so they got their money anyway. Charlotte was moved to a hospital in Tbilisi, where she received bedside visits from embassy officials and people from various state departments, although she was too doped up on sedatives to care. There was a formal apology, which meant less than nothing to her. Will didn't come. Nobody mentioned him. The baby moved inside her, turning and kicking, receiving a clean bill of health and an approximate date of conception. So many questions about when, where, why, but she was too tired to care about answers.

She wanted to forget. She just wanted to sleep.

* * * * *

"Dr. Mayfair?" A voice sounded from the back corner. "Dr. Mayfair? Is class over?"

A girl waved her hands in the front row of the classroom. Will's eyes focused and his mind came back to the present, which happened to be a beginning level Russian history class he'd taken over mid-semester. He'd been desperate for work, anything to take his mind off the rest of his life. He must have trailed off in the middle of a lecture. The students were staring like he'd grown a second head.

God, he had to give up the class, beg a sabbatical or resign for the time being. There were too many triggers in this work, too many reminders of that part of the world where he'd lost her. Charlotte, missing now for over four months. He counted each wretched day in his mind. He thought every hour of what had befallen her. Horrible, unspeakable acts.

He was afraid she wasn't alive.

If she were, they would have found her by now. Her mother and father put an astounding amount of money and manpower on the case from the second Will called them. They brought over private investigators and involved the State Department. Adyghe authorities bent over backward to help in the efforts, to find the renegade soldiers, to find the American woman who'd disappeared into thin air. Ivo flew over and stayed with Will in Krasnodar Krai, but the Rowes wouldn't meet with them. All offers of assistance from their quarter were ignored, and any attempts at contact rudely rebuffed.

Ivo suffered, but Will suffered more.

Will had known before he left the cursed clearing outside Aleronsk that it was too late for her. He'd driven with blood rushing in his ears to Maykop, ignoring the booms and sounds of gunshots, to a police station in chaos. The look they'd given him when he'd told the story only confirmed what he already knew. *This culture doesn't respect women.* He'd yelled at Charlotte about it one evening while he'd brushed her hair. He'd left Maykop, gunning for the embassy in Tbilisi. Hours of driving, hours to second-guess and worry and hate himself for leaving her.

My God. My God, what have I done?

He'd finally returned to London last month, only because he knew if he stayed over there trying to find her, he'd die. Not physically, but emotionally. Perhaps physically too. He couldn't concentrate on anything, couldn't sleep or eat properly. Couldn't teach worth a goddamn, that was for sure.

He dismissed the class and pulled up his email to send a letter of resignation to his department head. It was short and sweet. He wasn't into words much anymore. He finished it and pushed send before the last student had shuffled out of the class, then headed to his office to throw his things into the same box he'd used to bring them here a month before. There wasn't much. A few books and university manuals, which he'd leave for his successor, and a few files. The laptop was his own. He was just about to power it down and place it on top of the other things when an email notification popped up. Will clicked open his mail, wanting to get the whole dirty mess over with so he could go home and mourn and rage and wait for word of Charlotte. He would wait his entire life.

Or a second or two—the email wasn't from his boss, but his contact at the embassy. Will took a deep breath and scanned the text with his heart in his throat.

Dear Dr. Mayfair,

You will be pleased to learn that Charlotte Rowe was recovered last week in Shovgenovsky. She has been through an ordeal but by all accounts is in good condition. After a brief sojourn in a military hospital, she returned to the States. Miss Rowe asks for privacy at this time but will likely contact you soon regarding a personal matter.

I wish I could share more but I know very little. I hope you are doing well.

Best,

M. Dooley

Will went limp with relief. Euphoria followed, then grief. He felt a thousand emotions, so many emotions he fell on the floor for a moment and had to collect himself back up into the chair. He re-read the email again, trying to squeeze meaning out of the miserly phrases. The pivotal points burned in his brain. *Recovered. Ordeal. Good condition.* From those three phrases a world of imagined horrors sprang, but God, she was alive. She was in good condition, whatever that meant. Then there was the phrase, *will likely contact you.*

Likely? She had to contact him. He needed to see her, to touch her and prove to himself that she'd survived. What if she didn't contact him? What if she hated him as much as her parents, and refused to see him or speak to him ever again? It was what he deserved, but not something he could live with. And what did Dooley mean by "a personal matter?" Maybe she was going to sue him for his part in her ordeal. Reckless endangerment. Criminal negligence.

He wanted to go to her, to hold her, to unburden himself and apologize to her a thousand times. A million times, until she forgave him, if such a thing was possible. He waited and worried, writing back to Dooley several times and receiving no answer to his pleas for more news, only instructions to wait for further contact.

A week later, he woke to the front bell. A delivery man held out overnighted papers from the law offices of Goldman, Trask, and Riley. So she was suing him after all. At least he'd be able to see her again in court. He ripped open the envelope expecting to find a lengthy legal document but found only a one-page note.

Dear Dr. Mayfair,
Our client, C. Rowe, requests that you submit to a paternity test at your earliest convenience. Please have a physician of your choice contact our office to arrange this non-invasive medical procedure.
Respectfully,
Richard L. Riley, Esq.

Unlike the previous note, the meaning behind this message was easy to parse. For about thirty minutes he felt numb. It confirmed his worst fears while simultaneously bringing up a world of new ones. Pregnant!

But this wasn't about him, about getting his feet kicked from under him. Dear, organized Charlotte. This wouldn't be organized at all, no matter what happened.

Will took a couple days to tie up loose ends, packed the things he thought he'd need for the next few months, and bought a plane ticket to Savannah. He was afraid to face her, but there was nowhere else to go and nothing else to do. He had to go to her whether she wanted him or not.

Chapter Twelve: Real Tears

Will stared up at the palatial home of Charlotte's parents. The wide green lawn seemed an insurmountable obstacle. He'd flown all the way across the ocean from a rainy English winter to an unseasonably warm Savannah day so he could see her, and now he couldn't even step onto the walk. His wool suit jacket was back in the rental car with his luggage, but he still sweated. He steeled himself, crossed the vast green expanse, and lost his nerve again on the door step. He couldn't gather the courage to ring the bell.

Courage. He didn't have the right to use that word anymore. To even think it. How could he stand here falling apart after all Charlotte had been through? It was time to man up. He rang the doorbell and stood in his scratchy trousers and button-up shirt and tie. They were the clothes he'd bought to attend his granny's funeral a couple years ago. He was deep in mourning now.

An older version of Charlotte opened the door. Charlotte's mother, brittle and elegant, with Charlotte's balding father standing behind her. They both stared at him, undoubtedly aware of whom he was. Before he could speak, Charlotte's mother slapped him, a resounding crack across his cheek. It made the world go sideways for a moment. Mr. Rowe drew his wife away with a soft sound.

"Come in then," he said to Will. "Come into the parlor."

Will followed behind her parents to a beautiful, airy room near the front of the house. He couldn't picture Charlotte here amidst this luxury, not after their time in the cabin. At any rate, she wasn't here. He hadn't expected her to be. He sat on a sofa across from her parents, knowing he needed to say something, but not sure how to begin. So he began with the only words he could muster in the face of their accusing silence.

"I'm so, so sorry."

His cheek still burned from her mother's slap. He could feel the outline of her hand, each individual finger. They didn't speak, so he repeated himself.

"I'm so sorry. I stopped in Maykop but they couldn't help. I phoned the embassy and sped there as fast as I could, but she'd disappeared by the time we got back. We were too late. She was already gone by then."

He could barely eke out the last words. Excuses. Apologies. He could never exonerate himself. Her mother cried silently, a waterfall of tears shining on her face. A maid brought coffee and set it on the table between them, but no one touched it.

"If I could have... I would have done anything to save her from what happened. I would have done anything." Will paused, choking on regret. "I've gone over it a thousand times in my head. What I could have done differently. There were so many of...them..." He couldn't say the word *soldiers*. Couldn't say it to her parents. Couldn't even think it without feeling sick at the memory of facing them down, realizing he had to leave her with them. "I had to leave her. I had to get help. I thought—I thought it through and I thought it was my best chance."

"It was your only chance," Charlotte's father said gruffly. "In fact, you never had a chance. They were armed and you weren't. You were just one man."

"You shouldn't have been there in the first place," her mother cried.

"Now, Adele." Charlotte's father seemed an unlikely ally, but Will needed an ally at the moment. Gordon Rowe cleared his throat and put a hand to his brow. "This has been very difficult for my wife. For me too. For all of us."

Of course. How would Will feel toward a man who was ultimately responsible for the kidnapping and rape of his daughter? *Kidnapping. Rape.* As much as those words hurt to think about, Will preferred them to the words he'd feared for so many months. *We finally found her. She's dead.*

Will had known rationally, all along, that it was one or the other. Dead, or imprisoned by someone doing her harm. In some way he was thankful it was the latter. If she had died, he couldn't have seen her again. At least now he could see her, apologize to her—if she would listen to him. God, if she refused to see him... He had to get through her parents first, whatever it took. They had to let him speak to her. "Mrs. Rowe, Mr. Rowe, I'm so sorry for what happened. I don't know what else to say. I just... Please. I need to see her. Please." He clasped his hands in supplication.

They looked at each other. Charlotte's father said, "She doesn't want to see you."

"I can understand that, but I came all the way from London—"

"Oh, poor baby," her mother spat. "Are we supposed to feel sorry for you?"

"Adele," her father said, touching her hand.

"I quit my job," said Will. "I closed up my house and came here to stay as long as she needs me. I want to make amends."

Her mother looked like she had more to say, but Gordon squeezed her hand and she flattened her lips into a thin line.

"I know you didn't mean for this to happen," said Gordon. "But at the same time, you have to understand she's not the Charlotte you knew. She doesn't want to see you. She's...not the same."

Will paused, trying to think of what to say, and finally spread his hands in a helpless gesture. "I don't want to cause her more pain." He looked between them. "Is she here? Now? Is she at least physically recovered?"

"For the most part, yes." Her father's face tightened for a moment. "At the end, she hadn't eaten in over a week. She would have starved to death if those people hadn't gone through the man's papers. We came so close to losing her."

Adele began crying again. Will looked down at his hands, lacing his fingers together. "If I'd known where she was, I would have gone there and taken him apart with my bare hands, I swear it. When she got there, the first day, I tried to put her on a plane home. She wouldn't go. I'm not saying this is her fault," he said quickly, as Adele's eyes shot up. "But I wish I'd made her leave." He thought a moment. "No, I want to wish it, but I can't. I fell in love with her there. The truth is, I didn't want her to leave." His eyes blurred, so Adele and Gordon went a little fuzzy. "That's the worst part of it all. Even now, when I know I should leave her alone, I can't. Please," he said one last time.

They looked at each other, and for a moment Will was afraid they'd ask him to go, but then they stood together and led him through the house to the back door. Charlotte's mother reached for the doorknob. Mr. Rowe halted her and fixed Will with a look. "We'll give you some time alone. But we'll be right here if Charlotte needs us."

It was a warning. As soon as Charlotte wanted him to go, they would make him go. He couldn't think about that, couldn't think about her cutting him dead, sending him away. He opened the door and stepped out onto the patio. She was there, right there. The lovely shape and reality of her, the long hair and pretty profile he knew so well. She sat in a chair facing away from him, a shawl around her shoulders.

"Mama, I'm not hungry."

"Charlotte."

She stood and spun to face him, backing up a few steps. "What are you doing here?"

He couldn't tell whether it was hate or shock in her voice. It wasn't joy. He froze where he stood. She turned a little away from him and pulled her shawl closer.

"Charlotte—" The words he'd thought so many times, the apologies, the pleas choked in his throat.

"Why are you here?" she demanded again.

Will spread his arms. "I got the note from your lawyers. About a...a paternity test."

"You could have taken that anywhere." She glanced toward the door and lowered her voice. "I don't want my parents to know."

"To know you're pregnant?" he asked in confusion.

"No. To know it might be yours."

She was so thin and pale. So angry. He wanted to go to her, embrace her, but he didn't dare.

"I've been so worried," he said. "I'm sorry if it upsets you, but I had to see you, see that you were all right. I had to tell you—Charlotte—I'm so sorry. If I had known— If I thought—" She turned her back on him. His voice faltered. "I just wanted to apologize. I know it's not enough."

She spoke over her shoulder, as if she couldn't bear to look at him. "You want me to forgive you? Will you go away if I do? I don't want you here."

"Charlotte." It was all he could say. No, he didn't want to go away. Yes, he wanted to be forgiven, more than anything. He stared at her profile, searched her middle for a baby bump. She was a wisp. Wasted away. "Charlotte, I'm sorry."

"You knew that war was coming. You knew it wasn't safe."

"So did you," he said. "We both chose to stay. But I swear to God, if I had known—"

"You did know! You knew I wasn't safe there from the start. Why didn't you make me go? You should have made me."

"I thought we had more time." A lie. He amended. "I wanted more time."

"More time for your fucking language study. For your stupid stories."

"No. More time to be with you."

He heard the doorknob turn, heard it with some desperately attuned part of his brain. He waited to be thrown out, but no frowning parent materialized. *Thank you.*

"It wasn't about the language. The stories," he said in a softer voice. "Not at the end. You know it wasn't."

"It was about the fucking then."

"No."

"You kept me there for your own selfish benefit."

"You made the choice to stay." He would let her rail at him but he wouldn't let her rewrite history. She rubbed her forehead and gave a great, shuddering sigh.

"You should have made me go," she said. "Do you have any idea what I went through? What it was like to be trapped for months, powerless and terrified, waiting to die? I was sure I was going to die. Do you have any idea what it's like to live like that?"

He shook his head, unable to utter a word in the face of her pain.

She covered her face with her hands and then flung them down to her sides. "And I have this goddamn baby in me who will remind me of what happened until I can get rid of it." Her face twisted in anger. "But *you*—I can make you go away. I want you to leave and never come near me again. All I want from you is to know—"

Her voice cut off, but Will knew what she wanted to know. Whether the baby she was carrying was his or someone else's. At that point he wasn't sure it would make a difference. She was so agitated it frightened him. He wanted her to sit down. He wanted her to understand he would be there if she needed him. Either way, he would be there for her. "Charlotte, whatever you need, I'll do it. We'll face this together. Everything will be okay."

"I've heard that before. Forgive me if I don't believe you," she snapped as the patio door opened. Charlotte's mother appeared bearing a tray of coffee and cookies in a white-knuckled grip. She looked at Charlotte, but Charlotte was staring at the tray, her face a mask. Mrs. Rowe retreated silently.

"Oh, Charlotte," said Will. "I can't imagine what you've been through."

"No, you can't. No one can. It was that bad."

Her fury was better than apathy. He kept telling himself that. "What can I do? Just tell me. I'll do anything."

"Is that what you think? You can just do something and magically everything will be better? This isn't mythology. There's no magic to make this turn out differently." The shawl flew around her as she waved her arms.

"I wish you'd sit down."

"I wish you'd go away."

"I can't just go away and leave you!"

"You did before."

The words stabbed into him. He was mortally wounded, with no way to fight back except to burden her with his own pain. "Do you think it's been so great for me, the months you were gone? Do you think I've been blithe and happy, moving on with my life?" He crossed to her. She backed away, but he still came. "Do you think I haven't seen your face in every nightmare I've had? Heard your voice calling my name, like I could have fucking helped you?"

She looked stricken. He wanted to stop, but it spilled out like some gush of putrid bile. "I couldn't do anything. Do you know what that felt like? The horror, the helplessness? My only choice was to leave you, to go for help. I wish I could go back and do everything differently. Choose another region to study, a different culture, a different language group. Find a different translator to help me... Leave a week before we did. But I can't change any of it now."

He rubbed his eyes. There were no more tears to shed. There was nothing else to do. That was the awful thing about it. He gazed at her helplessly.

"I wish this never happened. I swear to God, I wish it with every fiber of my being. But if...can't we... Couldn't we... At least...?"

* * * * *

It was so bright in winter, with no leaves to shade them. That was why Charlotte's eyes were stinging. Not with tears. Not for him.

He sat so still. He'd scared her for a moment, waving his arms around and yelling. It reminded her too much of that night. It was easier to sit beside him at the table and stare off at her mother's hibernating rosebushes and the still, glassy pond.

It was just a pond, nothing like the grand lake at their campsite. There were no mountains ranging around in majestic splendor. Still, here he was. She'd wanted him and reviled him in cycles ever since that night she'd been shoved into the back seat of the military vehicle and thought, *oh shit, this isn't happening to me.* Even now, she wanted him to stay as much as she wanted him to leave.

He shifted, glancing down at the slight but clear evidence of her pregnancy. "So...you're having a baby?"

She had to give him chutzpah points for the casual delivery. "Yes. That would explain the request for your DNA. So we can tell if it's yours, or one of the soldiers who raped me." She said it to be cruel, but it was the truth.

Will blinked and rubbed his temple. "Well, what will you do if it's mine?"

"I don't know." She was silent a long while. "I dream sometimes that it comes out looking exactly like the man who held me prisoner, and I wake up screaming. If it's not yours, I'll give it up for adoption, I think. I'm pretty sure. My doctor says I'm not in any condition to be making decisions about it right now, that I should wait and think about things. If it's yours then...maybe...part of the decision should lie with you."

"You mean, whether to give it up for adoption?"

"Or, I don't know. You could keep it if you want. Him. It's a boy."

The baby shifted inside her, rearranging himself with a series of pokes. She put a hand over her womb, not that it ever quieted him. Will watched her, looking sad. "Are you attached to it at all? I mean...him?" He stared down at her belly. "Do you hate him?"

Charlotte didn't know how to explain. So many things in her life right now had two sides, love and hate. "When I was in that cabin, when I became aware he was with me...in a way, he was something in my life that wasn't evil. I loved him then. Or appreciated him. But whenever I thought about how he came to be—or how he possibly came to be—then I hated him for being half them. I also worried the pregnancy would give Damir the final push he needed to get rid of me, to wash his hands of the whole situation. So, I don't know. How I feel about him is complicated."

"Charlotte..." Will's voice trailed off.

"I wish you'd never come," she burst out. "We have nothing to talk about except..." Now she was the one trailing off. She vacillated between wishing to talk about it bluntly, as if it didn't matter to her, and teetering on the edge of tears. Her throat worked against sobs, but she was so tired of crying. Will gave her a sympathetic glance that almost shattered her.

"Why don't we just sit here together and not talk for a bit?" he said.

She fell into relieved silence. He scooted his chair closer, right next to hers, and poured coffee for them both. He reached for the sugar bowl.

"Sweets for the sweet," he murmured.

Two spoonfuls, three, before her resolve crumpled and tears eclipsed her sight. His arm came around her and she slumped against him, sobbing for sugar bowls and scribbled notes, for white gloves and dark mountains. For sparkling lakes and emerald forests and a reckless, charming linguist named Will. For lovely memories, and devastating ones that threatened to destroy her. For the growing baby she carried inside that she both loved and hated.

Later, after she calmed, there was an awkward regrouping. She wanted him to leave, but couldn't find the words to dismiss him so soon after she'd bawled against his neck. Will suggested a walk, enthusing about the foliage, the pond, all the idyllic scenery she took for granted, and Charlotte agreed, just because it was something to do.

It felt strange, walking around the gardens behind her parents' house with Will. Her grandfather had tended those gardens with her. She remembered running through the rosebushes, singing with him in the language he'd taught her, the dying dialect he'd worked so hard to teach her before she was even old enough to read. The worst that had happened to her back then was her hair getting caught on thorns and giving her a pull.

How things changed.

"How much longer to go?" Will asked. "Before the baby comes?"

"In the spring, they think. Early May."

"Has it been a difficult pregnancy, aside from the circumstances?"

"No." *Not as difficult as other things.* "I could sign adoption papers right now and wash my hands of it all," she said. "But even if the baby goes away..." She shrugged. "Even then I won't forget. So I don't know. I kind of agree with my doctor. I need time to think."

"That's probably wise. How soon can we know if it's mine?"

Charlotte turned to him. "What will you want? If it's yours?"

His expression was difficult to read. "I'm with your doctor. If it's mine, I'll need some time to think."

"The test won't take long to analyze. We can know by next week." She stopped at the edge of the garden, looking back at the house. "I don't want this to be some rapist's baby. I wish all the time for it to be yours."

"I've cried enough tears over this to get you pregnant ten times over." The allusion to the stories startled her. She frowned at him.

"Real tears, or the other?"

"Real tears, Charlotte." They began to walk again, back toward the house. "Ivo is so sorry, by the way. He begs your forgiveness."

Charlotte's thoughts toward Ivo weren't much kinder than her thoughts toward Will. "I guess he was disappointed not to get his translation."

"I gave him as much as you finished. He loved it. It wasn't worth it though, for what happened to you. We can find another text anytime. A thousand dying languages." He stopped beside a gnarled rosebush, picking at dry leaves. "Another Charlotte, not so much."

"Can you go to the lab tomorrow? For the test?"

"Of course."

"They'll take a swab from your mouth and compare your DNA to the amnio they did."

He nodded. "It will be good to know." He stared at her waist, at the faint bump of her pregnancy.

"Don't get too attached to it," she said, following his gaze. "Honestly, your chances aren't good." Not the most delicate way to put it, but she thought he should know.

He got a bright, fierce look in his eye. "Maybe if I sing a lullaby to him and tell him not to be mine."

Charlotte felt a smile crack the armor of her face. "That's such a stupid idea. Your singing isn't going to do anything but hurt my ears."

"You're the oracle," he said. "What do you think?"

Charlotte sobered, ran her hand over her belly.

"I have no idea. I really don't know. It was so soon after our...accident...that the other..." She couldn't seem to finish a complete sentence. "Well, the doctors couldn't tell," she said. "It happened too soon— In between—"

"It's okay. I understand," he said, looking away from her.

Awkwardness on top of heartbreaking memories on top of sadness. She wished he would go. It was hard to think of anything to say, because everything between them was a land mine. Everything they talked about either reminded her of what happened or broke her heart.

"When are you going back to London?" she asked.

"I don't know. It depends. I want to be here to help you."

She didn't want him in Savannah. She didn't want him hovering around while she tried to work her way through this. "I don't need your help," she said. "My parents are in massive protective mode. They can't bear to let me out of their sight."

"I don't blame them. They must have been..." His gaze dropped again to her belly, before flicking away. "Devastated."

Charlotte felt a chill, an awful suspicion. Did he hope the baby wasn't his? God, he was looking at her waist again. If he didn't want it to be his, she wished he would come out and say it. "You don't have to stay," she insisted. "You don't have to do anything. I actually wish you'd go home and get on with your life."

"What if the baby's mine?"

The question hung in the air between them. He wore that stubborn, piercing look she'd always hated, but she didn't have to deal with it now. Or ever. "Just go for the test," she said in tired dismissal. "Then we'll talk."

Chapter Thirteen:
Hard Questions

Will dreamed of Charlotte for five nights running, not dreams of anything specific. Just her warm hazel eyes and her myriad smiles. She had his phone number but she didn't call.

He'd gone to her obstetrician to take the test as soon as they could work him in. That was a humiliating experience. He wondered how much the staff knew about Charlotte's circumstances, because the nurse who administered the test scowled at him the whole time. They marked his name on the sample and promised results in five business days. On the fifth day Charlotte called at eight in the morning to tell him the results were available. At nine o'clock he was in her car on the way to the doctor's.

Of course. Why would she want to wait any longer than he did? Not that everything hinged on this one outcome. Either way, they had important things to discuss. But rationally, it *did* matter. Their discussions would be very different depending on the results of the test.

But God, for her to be right there again, sitting next to him, driving him through the streets of Savannah after he'd spent four months of his life with no idea where she was or whether she was alive. The racket of remorse and dread in his head had been silenced, a chorus of questions now chiming it its place.

"Is it safe for you to be driving?" he asked as she flew around a corner.

"I'm pregnant, not post-operational. I can drive up until the end, as long as I can fit a seat belt around myself."

She was self-sufficient here. In Adygea, she'd depended on him for everything, but here, she was terrifyingly independent. She could so easily send him away. He could leave and she would be perfectly fine without him. At one time, that thought would have pleased him. Now, it didn't seem so great.

"Thanks for letting me come along," he said.

She shrugged. "I'd need a court order to view the results without your permission."

"Oh, I see."

They were both stressed. This tension was okay. "The thing is," he said, "I don't want you to feel alone in this."

"I'm not alone. I go to counseling three days a week. I have an appointment after this so I can, you know, talk about the results, whatever they are."

"Can I come?" Will asked, only half joking.

"No."

They sat in the obstetrician's waiting room without speaking. Around them, other men and round-bellied women sat together and chatted. Some of the women had come alone. If he left, if the baby wasn't his and Charlotte sent him away, she would come here alone, probably, for the appointments that remained.

Sometimes the other men met his eyes for a moment. They surely assumed he was the father paired with the mother sitting next to him. Maybe I am, he thought to himself. He had a wild, irrational thought of bribing the doctor to say he was the father, to fake the test results if necessary. It would make things easier for her, and give him a reason to stay in her life whether she wanted him to or not. He wondered how much money it would take to grease a doctor. Probably more than he had.

It seemed an eternity before they were called. Charlotte touched his hand as they walked down the hall. "It's okay," she said. "This is part of the process, right?"

Part of the process—the process of Charlotte distancing herself from him. His fears and anxieties were nothing compared to what she'd endured, what she was still enduring, so he summoned up a smile of agreement. His palms felt sticky with sweat. He wanted to run away from this fraught consultation, but he couldn't. The doctor entered and looked at both of them, then sat behind his desk and slid a folded-over paper in his direction.

"Just so you know," the doctor said, "these tests are very reliable. The results were conclusive."

The doctor didn't look at him, which gave Will a sinking feeling in his gut. He opened the lab report, angling it so Charlotte could see. There were very few words, just a graphic chart in the middle. Blood rushed to his face and cheeks and his heartbeat accelerated as he searched for meaning in the printout. *William Mayfair is not excluded as the biological father of Baby Rowe.* What did that mean? Locus, alleles, combined parentage indexes... He scanned the table and the statements below until he hit on a phrase he understood. *Probability of paternity: 99.9900%*

He looked up at the doctor, then at Charlotte. She looked stricken. "This means he's mine, right? That I'm the father?" Will asked, just to be sure.

The doctor nodded and extended his hand. "Congratulations."

Will shook it and swallowed hard, then turned to Charlotte. Was she happy or sad?

The doctor looked between them in the awkward silence. "Well, I'll leave you two alone. Take as long as you need."

As long as we need for what? "It's good, isn't it?" he asked once the doctor left. He sounded like he was pleading.

The Edge of the Earth

"It is good." She bit her lip. "I'm sorry, I'm just so shocked. I didn't think..." She put a hand over her mouth, then looked up at him with brimming eyes. "I wished so much for it to be yours. You can't even imagine."

Oh, but he could imagine. He took her hands and held them gently. "It's wonderful news. I would love to hug you, but I don't know if it's okay. Can I hug you?"

A long, excruciating pause and then, "No. Not just now."

He pulled his hands away from her, grasped the armrests of his chair.

"I'm sorry," she said. "I need time, that's all. I need space."

"It's okay. I understand."

"But I am glad. I'm glad it's yours. I just don't know what that means yet."

"Neither do I," he said slowly.

"Can I take this to my session?" She picked up the printout.

"Sure. I don't think I'll forget what it says anytime soon."

She ignored his lame joke and looked at her watch. "I'd better drive you back to your hotel so I can make my appointment."

"I can take a cab." It sounded sharper than he intended. "I don't want to make you late."

She looked at her watch again. Will didn't know what he'd expected. Happiness, jubilation. A celebration. Not this emotionless reaction.

"I have time," she said.

He shook his head, forcing a taut smile. "No, I'll get myself home. Your session is more important. When you've had the time and space you need to think about things, give me a call."

* * * * *

Charlotte drove around downtown for thirty minutes in a daze. She knew she'd hurt Will's feelings. She didn't care. At least she told herself that. It occurred to her he'd turned his life upside down to come see her, so she felt bad that she didn't want him there, but she didn't. She wondered what would happen if she never called his number again. Would he leave?

No, he wouldn't leave, not again. That was the whole thing about this. He'd left her once. He would stay now until the bitter end to redeem himself, especially since the baby was his. She felt so conflicted, so confused. Even though it was the result she'd wished for, she hadn't expected it. Jesus, what were the chances?

Then again, what were the chances that she'd speak some rare dialect, and that he and his partner would uncover that book, and that Ivo would find her in Savannah, and that she'd fly across the world and end up chained to a wall for four months, barely cheating a slow, solitary death? Charlotte shuddered and glanced over at the folded test results sticking out of her purse. *Probability of paternity: 99.9900%* That was a sure thing. No chance involved, not anymore.

Charlotte didn't know why it had hit her so hard. She should be happy, overjoyed that the baby inside her wasn't some rapist's. That it didn't belong to Rado Damir, the man who'd almost taken her life.

She arrived at her counselor's office on time and promptly broke down. She cried more than she talked, and certainly didn't come to any decisions about next steps. What she liked about her counselor was that Marjorie was okay with her crying and saying "I don't know. I don't know. *I don't know.*" Because Charlotte just didn't know.

"This is part of the process," Marjorie said. Marjorie talked about "the process" a lot, and it gave Charlotte hope, because it made it sound like there was some inevitable end in sight. A process would lead to a result—Charlotte moving on with her life and feeling okay. That was the hope anyway, that she'd escape from the questions and confusion and doubt and crippling fears. "You cry as much as you want," Marjorie nodded. "Until things seem clearer."

Charlotte wished the process was over, that it didn't spread out before her for days and months and years. She figured it would take years to come to terms with what happened to her, and perhaps her entire life now that the baby was his. With Will in her life—and Will's son, for God's sake—how could she move on from her past?

She felt defeated at the outset. Trapped.

Her continued strategy was avoidance. She didn't call Will for a week, and he didn't try to contact her. A week turned into two weeks, and the baby started moving inside her with new energy, pummeling athletic kicks resonating in her womb. It was like the baby insisted she get her ass in gear and do something to move forward, like calling his father and figuring out what the hell was going on.

Charlotte knew she needed to talk to Will. Even Marjorie said so, but she didn't push her to follow through. Charlotte stared at his phone number at least once a day and did everything possible to put off the conversation they'd have to have, even when she started to feel better. The third week, she moved out of her parents' house and back to her own place. She returned to work, which she found extremely therapeutic. In some part of her mind, she knew she was doing it to prove she didn't need Will. Except she was afraid that maybe she did.

Maybe he'd already left. *No, he won't leave you, Charlotte. And you shouldn't be ignoring him.*

But it pains me to be with him.

And it pains me to be without him.

"Charlotte? Earth to Charlotte."

Charlotte looked up from her ongoing inner dialogue into Roger's patient gaze.

"Are you sure you're ready to come back to work, boss?"

"Yes, I'm sure."

"Because I can hold things together a little longer. As long as you need. Just sayin.'"

She glared at him. "Are you 'just sayin'' you don't need me?"

Roger chuckled as Charlotte walked around the living room of the contemporary loft they'd organized, stopping to twitch a velvet sofa pillow a bit to the left.

"Oh, that's much better," Roger said out of the corner of his mouth.

"I only pick at your pillows because they're too perfect otherwise." As if to prove her point, she twitched the same pillow back the way he'd had it.

He watched her thoughtfully. "I know you like things perfect."

She started walking again, so tired of being the focus of his assessing looks, his worry. Everyone looked at her that way. She wandered into the foyer, admiring a handsome wooden coat rack. "I can never thank you enough, Rog. For keeping everything together while I was...away."

"It was nothing. You left everything so organized, all I had to do was let the business run itself."

"That's not true. You've been working really hard. I can see it in your face."

He clapped two hands to his cheeks. "No! Wrinkles? Dark circles?"

Charlotte laughed. "Vain as ever. It's nice to know some things never change."

She circled back into the kitchen and dining area. It would be alive later with a grateful family, making use of neatly organized cabinets and countertops. God, she'd missed this work.

"So what's next on the agenda?" she asked.

"A couple houses in Midtown, and one in Hudson Hill. The team can handle it if—"

"I love Hudson Hill."

"Let's do Hudson Hill then." He looked at his watch. "Tomorrow."

"So you have plans for tonight? How's Perry these days?"

He leaned against the counter. "What are you avoiding? Standing here small-talking with me?"

"I'm not avoiding anything." It sounded like a lie. She shrugged and half-turned from her assistant. "Okay, it's Will. You remember, the one who..."

"I remember."

"So..." She gestured loosely at her waistline. "This baby is his."

Roger's eyebrows rose the slightest bit before falling back into place. "I didn't know."

"We found out a few weeks ago, but since then I've been avoiding him and I feel bad about it. I don't even know..." She swallowed hard. "I'm not even sure he's in Savannah anymore. Which I guess is okay."

Roger studied her face. "So, you don't care that he's the father?"

"No, I do. I mean..." She sat on a bar stool and leaned back to look at the cathedral ceiling. "I have no idea what happens now."

"Have you talked to him about it?"

"We talked about it in general terms. Before we knew. But now that I know, it all seems a lot more confusing. I mean, it happened accidentally. The pregnancy. The baby."

Roger looked shocked. "How did someone as cautious and controlling as you get knocked up?" He waved a hand. "Sorry, did that sound rude? I don't know whether to offer congratulations or a lecture on safe sex."

"You're about to get fired."

Roger composed his face and pretended to look apologetic. "So it's his baby, and yours. And this all happened...before..."

"Yes, before."

"But then..."

"Yes."

He nodded sagely. "I see. Yes, that's fucked up. How does he feel about all this?"

She shrugged. "He claims he'll do whatever I want, but I don't know his honest feelings. Whether he really wants to be in the baby's life, or whether he's doing it out of, you know..."

"A sense of obligation?"

"Yes."

Roger crossed to sit beside her. "What about him being in *your* life? Do you like him? Do you want him to be part of your future?"

"I don't know. It was kind of all...his fault." But it wasn't. She knew it wasn't, and so did Roger. They'd already had that talk. "Part of me loves him and part of me hates him. I guess that's the crux of the thing. Can the love part win over the hate part? And how do we get to that place? What if we *don't* get to that place?"

Roger sidearmed her into a hug. "You'll handle it either way, Char. And you know I'll be here to help however I can. You'll have lots of friends and family to support you in raising the baby, even if you and he don't work out."

"But..." Her face fell. "That's the thing. I wish we could work out."

"Who says you won't?"

"With the way things began? How could we?"

Roger tsked. "How a relationship starts doesn't matter. What matters is how it continues. Tell me this, does he love you?"

It was a brutal question. Just the sort of question she depended on him to ask.

"I don't think so. I think he would stay with me out of a sense of duty, but marriage and family isn't something he's ever wanted. And you know..." She looked around at the flowers, the rich carpet, the symmetrical candles on the kitchen island. "I never wanted kids either."

"I remember. Too messy and disorganized."

She buried her head in her hands. "I don't know how I'm going to do this."

"Oh, girl," Roger said, stroking her hair. "It will all work out."

"I feel so out of control. No matter what happens, I'm afraid I'll be miserable. And I know it's stupid, that I should be grateful to be here at all—"

"Wait, wait! Who says you're going to be miserable? You're in a crazy situation, but that doesn't mean you can't make some happiness out of it."

"It's not just me though. Will is involved. And this...this baby," she said, gesturing to her waist. "And there's all this guilt and bad memories between us. Everything's all screwed up. My life, my feelings. My relationships and the life I imagined for myself, all blown to hell, and I can't stand how that feels."

"Honey, sometimes you need to let go and ride the whitewaters of life."

"I hate whitewaters," she whined.

"I know, but it is what it is. It's too bad I can't take you out for a drink to drown your sorrows. You could probably use a real bender about now."

She nodded and laughed softly, pulling away from him. "Maybe after. In a few more months." *But you'll be a mother then.* Would she be? Or would she give the baby away and pretend it never happened, shove it all into some forgotten place? "God, I don't know what I'm doing. I don't know what to do, Roger."

"Have you told Will that?"

"No. I don't want him to think I'm not strong enough. I want him to feel like he can leave if he wants to."

"Have you told him you love him?"

Charlotte blinked and stared at her friend. "I don't...well... No."

Roger shrugged and picked at an invisible piece of lint on his pants. "I can't say I know everything that makes you hetero folks tick, but that might be a starting place. It might make things a little clearer for both of you if you fessed up to all these emotions you're feeling."

Charlotte looked down, twisting her hands. "I can't. I'm too scared. I'm a coward."

He shook his head. "Not a coward. Just someone who's used to being in control. And love is never about control." He waved a finger under her nose. "You need to talk to him, either in English or that weird Apache language you know together, and tell him what's in your heart."

* * * * *

She called out of the blue, on a Tuesday afternoon. She didn't say much, only asked if she could come to his hotel. Will agreed at once, then went down to wait for her in the lobby, not knowing if this would be the first of many visits, or the last time he'd see her.

It didn't take her long to arrive. As she walked toward him, he noticed that she'd gone from very thin and barely pregnant to healthier and visibly pregnant in the space of a few weeks. She was still wearing regular clothes that hugged her bump, not those blousy maternity things.

Did women even wear those anymore? He never looked at pregnant women. They'd never been on his radar before. Now they were. This one at least.

"I'm sorry I didn't call—" she started at the same time he said, "It's good to see you."

They both stopped and stared at each other amidst the mod-depressing pleather sofas and round glass tables of the hotel lobby.

"I'm sorry I didn't call you," she said again. "I should have called but I didn't know what to say. I still don't know what to say."

You didn't have to say anything. A simple acknowledgement of my existence would have been nice. He wasn't mad at her. He was trying not to be, anyway. He looked down at her belly, outlined so clearly by her tight red tee. "I would have liked to hear from you sooner, but I understand you had some thinking to do." He paused and looked at her sideways. "Were you thinking?"

"Yes. Were you?"

"About a million things."

A family walked by them, their kids racing to push the elevator button first. An older couple argued on a nearby sofa while a small group of college students debated where to eat. Will looked at Charlotte.

"Do you want to go upstairs? It would be more private there. I guess we have things to talk about. Isn't that why you came? To talk?"

"Yes. We need to talk." She looked a bit woebegone. They ended up on the elevator with the family, but the kids were too busy fighting over the buttons to notice when Charlotte started to cry. She hid her face against his shoulder until the noisy family got off, and then she turned to him and let him hold her. They weren't loud, dramatic tears, just quiet ones. When they got to the twelfth floor, he led her to his room. He held her inside the door, soothed her until she calmed down.

"I'm sorry for ignoring you," she said. "I feel so bad. I've been afraid of seeing you. I was afraid you might be gone."

"Don't be afraid," Will said, although he was personally terrified. Even holding her was a trauma, because he wanted her. Even now, after everything, he wanted her. Not just because she was lovely, but because she was sad and hurting. He wanted to lay her down, taking care with her gently rounded belly, and use his skill to erase what these last months had wrought. He wanted to bring her out of the dark forest she'd gone into so it was nothing but a distant memory.

"I'm okay." She pushed away from him, averting her gaze. She wiped off the last of her tears, holding herself away from him in a way he couldn't misinterpret, his Charlotte, who he'd made love to with such abandon. She clearly had no intention of rekindling that flame, which was perfectly okay.

"So," she said, looking around. "You've been living in a hotel all this time?"

"They have a weekly rate. I'm going to stay here until… Well, until the baby comes anyway. I guess that's what we really need to talk about." Her hands went to her waist. Will stared, unable to hold back the words anymore. "Can I touch it?"

She looked surprised he would ask, but she nodded. He put a hand over her middle, tentatively at first, then both hands. He cradled the bump of her belly like a globe, the earth between his palms.

"I'm glad it's mine," he said, opening his fingers. "I really am, Charlotte. I think everything's going to be fine. So I don't think you should cry or be scared or worried. I don't want you to be worried." He stopped fondling her belly, let his hands fall to his sides. "Did you spend the last few weeks worrying?"

"I spent the last few *months* worrying," she said. "And now I have all these new things to worry about. I'm worried about what you're thinking, whether you really want this baby."

"Does it change anything if I don't?"

"You don't want it?"

He sighed. "I didn't say that. I'm here, aren't I?"

"You didn't cry."

"What?"

"When we got the paternity results. You didn't cry."

"I would have cried if I hadn't been trying so hard to figure out that goddamn table. Anyway, you didn't cry either."

"I was too shocked to cry."

He had a sudden, vivid memory of her standing in the door to the bathroom, bursting into tears over tangled hair and newfound vulnerability. She was such a different woman now. More seasoned, more beautiful. Hardened a little, but softened too, as if the tragedy she'd endured had given her a new armor of wisdom. She looked worldly-wise, nothing like the Charlotte who'd complained about spiders and the lack of a shower, and the pitfalls of casual sex.

She walked past him, over to the window to look out. He wondered if she'd notice what was on the table beside her, what had occupied his time while he waited for her to call. When she did, she took a step backward.

"Oh my God," she breathed. "You still have it."

"I still have it," he said. The stolen document from Adygea, sitting open on his hotel room table. He hadn't had the heart to get it out until he'd seen her at her parents', alive and well.

"Wow." She came closer, staring down at the mottled cover, and the stack of her notebooks. "I never thought about what happened to them until now."

"I brought them home. It was a little dicey when I flew out of Rostov. They went through my luggage, but they didn't look in my briefcase."

She sat down at the table. "No one ever reported it missing?"

He shook his head, sitting on the other side. "The museum was destroyed in the fighting," he said. "Looted and burned down, like I suspected."

"Oh. That's sad."

"So I haven't given it back. Obviously. Not yet."

"They must assume it was destroyed with the rest of the antiquities." Charlotte reached out to trace the cover. No gloves, but he let her touch. If anyone had earned a grope of the book, it was Charlotte. She looked up at him. "You could probably keep it now."

"I will, for a while." He straightened the corners of her notebooks, squaring up the edges. "But it would be nice for them to get it back. It's nice to get something back you thought was lost forever."

She looked away, opened the top notebook and leafed through her scrawled handwriting. He remembered so many nights going back and forth with her, her pencil tap-tap-tapping while she tried to find the exact right word. His beautiful lens who'd worked so hard. In the end that was why he'd pulled the book out and started working again, even though it hurt his heart.

She paused with one of the notebooks in her hand, running her fingers across the ragged cover, the dog-eared pages. "They seem like a relic. Something from ages ago."

Oh, Charlotte, you don't know...you just don't know. "I thought you were dead," he blurted out. "I wanted to destroy the document, tear it to pieces. I thought they would never find you. That these notebooks would be all I had of you."

"You thought I was dead?"

"Yes."

She stared at the notebook in her hand, and he wished he hadn't spoken of it. He bit his tongue against saying more.

"I thought of you a lot there," she said.

"About how much you hated me?"

She looked pained. "No."

"I thought maybe you'd died wondering why I didn't try to help you. Why I let them take you."

"I knew why."

"I went for help."

"I know."

"I thought it was the best choice. I had analyzed it all in my head."

"Will."

"While he was talking, I was going crazy thinking what to do, the best way to help you. I thought that was the best choice, to go for help, but now I don't know. I thought if I had tried harder, I could have found some other way."

"Will." She put her hand over his on the table. "There was no other way."

"We should have stayed at the cabin. I should have taken the gun at least. There was a gun in the cabin, under my bed. I never told you. I didn't want to scare you. God." He pulled his fingers from hers and buried his head in his hands. "I should have fought harder. I should have promised them money. If I'd offered them money— But I didn't even think of it. If I knew—" He choked a little, falling apart. Coming apart at the seams, now. Complete disintegration. "If I'd known what they were going to do to you— If I'd known, I never would have left you."

"Will." Her soft voice silenced him. She came around the table and cradled his head in her hands.

"I knew, Charlotte." The confession spilled out, and the tears, drowning him. "I knew what would happen to you. I knew what they were going to do. Oh God, the look on your face when I closed the door and drove away." He clutched at her, hiding his face in her side, ashamed, hating himself. She stroked his hair in a calming, gentle rhythm.

"It's okay. I'm right here and I'm fine now. Let go of it. You've suffered enough."

"I can't. I can't let it go. And how can you say you're fine?" he asked, looking at her belly. "I did this to you. All of this is my fault."

She pulled away from him. "What's done is done. So you got me pregnant. At least it was you and not them." She squared her shoulders, as if she expected him to protest. "It's a baby, not cancer or ebola. This," she said, pointing to her belly, "is not curable, but it's not fatal either. So I would appreciate if you would stop treating me as if I actually died over there."

He stared at her. "I'm not treating you like you died."

"You aren't treating me like a survivor either. I can't live in that time anymore, okay? I don't want to think anymore about what happened that night, or any of the nights after. I want to put my life back together again. I want to be happy again. Will, I really forgive you. Let it go. It's time to move on with your life too."

She left him and sat back down, leafing through her old notes.

Will sat still, blindsided and panicking. "But...what about the baby?"

"What about him?"

"When you say it's time for me to move on with my life...do you mean...without you?"

She looked down, picking at a corner of one dog-eared page. "You told me you weren't family-man material."

"I said that a lifetime ago."

"It was less than a year ago."

"A lot has changed since then." He stalled, trying to read her, but she gave him nothing. "What do you want? Do you want me to stay with you? Maybe we ought to stay together if it's our baby. Give the family thing a try."

"Do you want to be a husband? A father?"

Damn. She asked the hard questions. *I don't know if I want to be a husband or father. But I'd try it, for you. To not lose you. Is that enough?* "I think we could make a pretty good life together. You, me, and a baby. We could figure things out."

She slid him a skeptical look. "You live across the ocean from me."

"We could figure things out," he insisted. "We could make things work."

"Maybe." She couldn't have sounded more noncommittal. She closed the notebook and put it down. "Maybe we should keep going with the document. While you're here. We were so close to finishing."

Will stared at her and swallowed hard. "Would you want to?"

"I'm kind of bored in the evenings, sitting around growing more and more massive."

She was the farthest thing from massive. And God, he would love to work with her again, if it meant she was feeling better. That she was ready to put her life back together and move on. "I'd love to work some more," he said. "If you want to. You don't have to, though, really."

Charlotte shrugged and smiled at him. God, that smile. It seemed like a thousand years ago that he'd laughed and held her close with no tragedy between them. A thousand years since their work on the stories had fallen away. She dropped her eyes and then lifted them again, spreading her fingers on the stack of notebooks.

"Yes, I would like to. I'd really like to know how it all ends."

Chapter Fourteen: I See You Well

Charlotte sat up in bed with a gasp. Another too-vivid nightmare. *It's okay. You're okay.* The nights were hard because it was dark and she was alone, and it made her remember the dark nights in her cabin prison. Leaving the lights on didn't help because it was still dark outside, and Rado Damir still came to her in her sleep.

She pulled her blanket closer around her. Sometimes if she stayed awake a while before she slept, the nightmare wouldn't come back, the nightmare of the key in the lock and his face at the door. Or worse, the nightmare of no key in the lock for days and nights and days and nights on end while hunger gnawed at her and she waited for death. She looked at the clock. It was too late to call anyone, but she really wanted to call Will.

Since she'd finally summoned the courage to talk to him, something inside her had started healing. It was a big step out of her "victim space" as Marjorie would say. The conversation had been wrenching and emotional, but it comforted her to know he planned to be there for her through thick and thin. It took a lot of questions away. The only thing was, she didn't want him to stay with her out of a sense of guilty duty, then realize twenty years down the road he'd thrown away his life on a woman he didn't love. She didn't want him to have regrets. She didn't want to trap him with guilt.

But she did want him, as she'd told Roger. Not sexually. She couldn't think of sex yet without shuddering, but when she was with Will she felt emotionally safe, like he was the only man on earth she could trust not to hurt her. He was definitely the one person who could understand her, really understand all she'd been through. *It's too late to call*, she chided herself as she dialed his number.

"Hello? Charlotte, what is it?"

She blinked. The concern in his voice almost made her cry.

"It's nothing," she said. She couldn't tell him about the nightmares without falling apart completely. "I— I couldn't sleep."

A pause, and then a gentle "Why not?"

She could have told him about the nightmares then. He was inviting her to open up to him, in his light, non-threatening way. "I was thinking that— You're living in a hotel," she sputtered instead.

"Yes. It's okay. I got a weekly rate."

"You said that already." His damn weekly rate. It was so much money, so much sacrifice on his part to remain by her side.

"Charlotte, are you crying?"

"No," she sobbed.

"I can hear that you're crying, actually," he said in his silly, proper English accent.

"Then why did you ask if I was?" she snapped, her voice cracking on the last word. "Why don't you come here?" Her voice rose in a kind of fury. "You shouldn't be staying in a hotel when I have two extra rooms at my place. I think you should come stay here."

He was silent a moment and she was afraid he'd say no, and she'd have to stay alone through night after dark night, just the nightmares and her. But he didn't say no. He said, "Do you need me to come right now? Tonight?"

She looked at the clock. It was two in the morning. "Yes," she bawled. "I want you to come tonight. But I don't want to sleep with you."

"You don't have to sleep with me."

"I thought maybe we could work at night, like we did at the cabin. And you won't have to pay for the hotel."

"I'm already packing," he said. "I'll be there in a bit. Do you want me to stay on the phone with you?"

"Yes. Please."

So he stayed on the phone with her, all through the hour it took him to pack and check out and ride across town in a taxi in the middle of the night. She said that he'd have to buy more minutes for his pay-as-you-go cell phone, but he said he didn't care. She used all those minutes to tell him about the nightmares, the way Rado Damir invaded her sleep and the way it felt when he didn't come and the sun moved across the floor of the cabin through the crack under the door. She told him about captivity, and the horrible ache for freedom, the thoughts of turning liquid so she could slide out of her bonds and under the door into the light. She told him all the things she couldn't burden her parents and Roger or even Marjorie with.

He didn't hang up until she answered the door and then she felt an almost numbing relief. Moving out of her victim space didn't mean all her fears disappeared, or that her memory was erased. It didn't mean she was strong all the time. She helped him carry his luggage up from the taxi and put it in the guest room next to hers. Then he hugged her in the hall while she cried for bad nightmares and good friends whose accidental babies you were carrying. When she finally stopped crying he said he'd leave his door open, and she should too so he could hear if she needed him. The rest of that night, though, she had no more nightmares.

Instead, she had bright and elaborately detailed dreams about Will and Lady Satanay sipping tea on the shore of a glistening lake, with mountains undulating in the distance and reaching for the clouds.

* * * * *

Will lay awake a long time after she slept, finding Charlotte's house spookily quiet after the noisy environment of the hotel. No whirring of the elevator, no creaking of the bed. Charlotte's guest bed was nirvana after the rock he'd slept on. He supposed that was what you got for a weekly rate.

After her anger, after the divide that had separated them for so long, they were connecting again. They hadn't made any definite decisions, but he felt assured she wasn't going to cut him off completely, which had been his greatest fear. Quite the opposite, she was allowing him back into her life. He'd touched the swell of her belly, rested his hands right over their baby. He'd expected her bump to feel soft but it felt hard as rock. God, she was so strong. How had he never seen it?

Because she kept giving in to you.

When he woke in the morning she was gone. She'd left a note that she'd be working with her assistant until four. Will wasn't sure it was good for her to be working so hard, especially when she couldn't sleep at night, but he knew her business was important to her, and she looked healthy enough. Based on her disjointed but insightful monologue on the phone the night before, he thought her counseling sessions were helping, and work probably helped too.

He also had work to do, very important work. He realized that if he didn't finalize an exhaustive record of the dialect, if he didn't publish papers and at least one volume of the stories, all Charlotte's suffering would have been in vain, and he couldn't live with that.

But first he would poke around her home while she was away and touch her things like a stalker. He couldn't help himself. Charlotte was still such a mystery to him, this woman who was carrying his child, this woman he felt closer to than any other woman in his lifetime. This woman he hadn't known a year before.

Her condo wasn't huge, nothing like her parents' palace. Living room, kitchen, small dining table off to the side of the kitchen. Three bedrooms and two baths. One of the bedrooms served as an office for her business, and had the name and logo on the door. *OrganizeNation, Inc.*

He looked in and found the space as neat and well-organized as he expected it to be. It seemed strange that her company had gone on accepting jobs, even growing, the whole time she was away. There was a collage of work-related photos pinned to a corkboard that took up an entire wall. So many sleek, uncluttered kitchens and perfectly arranged play rooms. There were rows of handwritten thank you notes, along with photos of happy families. Charlotte wasn't in any of the snapshots. She was behind the camera, no doubt.

The other bedroom was a guest room—his room—neutral but comfortable with heavy, antique wooden furniture. It had a bumped-out window seat overlooking a small, neat yard. He immediately thought, *this would make a great nursery*. Never, ever had he considered himself a candidate for fatherhood. He still didn't, but some reckless part of him wanted to try. And marriage... How many times had he bragged to his friends, *I'll never settle down with one woman*. He'd left it to his sisters to marry and provide the grandchildren. His mother had seven of them so far. She'd soon have eight.

He couldn't remember now why he'd been so against marriage and children. Some tiring relationships in his twenties. A broken heart when he thought he'd found "the one," and then the segue into the travel lifestyle, where long-term unions didn't make sense. Honestly, he'd enjoyed the freedom of friends-with-benefits relationships and one night stands. He'd enjoyed living selfishly, living only for himself. Until now.

He drifted into Charlotte's bedroom last. Her bed was hysterical, raised and fluffy, with a ruched, beribboned mess of a counterpane and tiers of ruffles cascading down the sides. It was stacked with embroidered pillows. He sat on the edge of it, toying with the frilly embellishments. This was where she belonged, her princess's bower. What must she have thought of their mountain cabin? What would she think if she saw his austere London flat, barely maintained in habitable order between his numerous trips afield?

He wandered around, looking first at the photos and notes on her meticulously arranged bulletin board. The unused push pins were stored in a straight line down one side. So Charlotte. There were symmetric photo collages and shelves full of books arranged by size, romance novels mostly. He looked down at the embracing couple on the cover of one and smothered a smile. No wonder she had such romantic notions about relationships. He put the book back and looked to the right. Three antique china dolls slumped against one another on her bureau. They all had hair the color of Charlotte's, and her impish smile too.

He picked up the largest one and looked down at the doll's expressive face. He turned it over and back, his clumsy fingers smoothing the yellowed linen dress. He put it down and noticed a small gilded frame partly obscured by the cluster of doll skirts. It was a photo of Charlotte as a child, sitting in an old man's lap. It had to be her grandfather.

The old man had a hint of the Caucasus in him, in his light eyes and the shape of his face. Charlotte looked off to one side, distracted, her wild hair tied with vivid-colored scarves. She too looked impossibly Circassian. The child in the photo laughed, a miniature version of the woman he knew today. Will stared, enthralled. It was impossible not to smile at the girl she was. But his smile faded as he ran a finger over the words engraved at the bottom of the frame: *My Princess.*

Will put the frame back and rearranged the smiling dolls beside it. It was wrong to snoop around her bedroom while she was away. He went back to the kitchen and opened the refrigerator to find something to make for breakfast...er...lunch. Man, he'd really slept in. He pulled out some things to make a sandwich and closed the door. The small magnetic words on Charlotte's freezer caught his attention.

I AM SO BORED

What had she told him, that first day when he'd picked her up at the airport? *I'm ready for some adventure.* She had flown there in search of adventure, and stayed even when he told her she ought to go home. He realized she was right, that blame and regret were pointless now. They had both made missteps, and they had both paid a price for them. They had had some wonderful times as well.

He would try his damndest to make wonderful times again.

* * * * *

When Charlotte got home each night, they ate dinner and then worked together on the manuscript, just as they had at the cabin. Well, not exactly the same as at the cabin. He didn't come on to her now, didn't flirt and act like a jackass the way he had back then. They were way past that now. Will still wanted her as much as he ever had, perhaps more, now that she seemed so wise and strong. When they worked on their stories he imagined her as Lady Satanay, as the Tree Lady, as all the strong women and goddesses in the myths.

As strong as she seemed, Will knew she still struggled. She tossed and turned most nights, and cried out in her sleep. He always stood by her door until he was sure she'd settled. The second week, she had a full-on, screaming night terror. He ran into her room, certain she was being murdered. He gathered her up and held her until she woke enough to stop fighting him. "It's okay," he whispered over and over. "You're okay now."

She buried her face in his chest, sobbing against his faded tee shirt. "He came back for me again. It felt so real this time. He was dragging me to that cabin and I couldn't fight him. I couldn't wake up!"

"He's never coming back." Will stroked her hair, hugging her close until she quieted. "You're safe now, love. He can't get to you, not ever again."

"Don't go." Her fingers curled around his arms. Her whole body shook and shuddered.

"I won't leave. Not until you tell me to," he promised.

"Lay down with me." She pulled him to the bed beside her. It wasn't sexy talk, a come-on. It was an order from a distraught person, and he obeyed. They huddled together face to face, her ever-growing bump between them. She timed her breathing to his, or maybe he timed his to hers. Her face relaxed. Her gaze traveled over his chest, his arms, then back up to his face.

"Better now?" he asked softly.

"Better. For now."

"Should I go?"

She ignored his question and asked instead, "Do you believe in God?"

Will had to think about that a moment. "It's complicated for me. I know about a lot of gods because I've studied a lot of cultures. People find solace in their gods, and I think that's a good thing. One thing I've learned is that deep down, all people are the same. They all ask the same questions and seek the same answers. They crave the reassurance of a deity, the knowledge that the mysteries and sorrows of the universe are out of their hands. What's funny is how some gods are frightening and others are nurturing, depending on the various cultures. There are even comical gods."

"You're a talker, Will," she sniffed. "I just wanted a yes or no."

"Then my answer is maybe."

She laughed, turning away from him a little. "Do you ever wonder what dying feels like? I mean, you know, the process?"

He stared at her profile, trying to read her. "Why are you asking me this?"

"Sometimes I dream that I'm dying, but I always wake up before it happens, and I think it might be because I don't know what it would feel like. Whether it hurts, or maybe feels like nothing at all."

"I guess it would depend on how you died. This is a pretty grim conversation, by the way."

"I'm sorry."

"It's okay. I just hope if you were— If you felt—"

She turned back to him. "I'm not going to kill myself. I came too close to 'been there, done that' to throw in the towel now."

"Oh, Charlotte." Without really meaning to, he put his arms around her and bent his head to hers. Not to kiss her, just to be close to her. Their foreheads touched and they lay still together, two people who were very much alive.

"I think you only know how it feels to die when you die," he said. "Then you get to experience what comes after."

"What if nothing comes after?" she asked.

"Then hopefully you enjoyed your life. I think the most important question isn't how death feels, because that will be over in a short time. The most important question is how your life feels."

Her eyes were two points of light in the darkness. "That's a pretty interesting way of looking at it."

"I try to be interesting." He paused and touched his nose to hers. "Speaking of interesting, there's this language called Ubykh. It has eighty-one consonants, but only three vowels."

He could feel more than see Charlotte's smile. "I heard about that once before. From this crazy linguist guy."

"And it was never written down, not anywhere. Only spoken. It didn't have a written form."

"I know." She blinked a little and touched his lips. "Stop. You'll make me cry."

"Thank you for letting me be in your life," he said past her fingers.

She took them away and ducked her head. "Thank you for taking care of me."

Better late than never. The offhand remark banged right into his head, but he suppressed it because this wasn't a moment for offhandedness.

Thank God for second chances, he thought instead, to whatever God was out there. If he believed in anything, he believed he was meant to be exactly here, with Charlotte, at this very moment. If there was nothing else, this was enough for him. Him and Charlotte, safe, together on her ruffled princess bed.

Chapter Fifteen: Perseverance and Bravery, and Love

The days eased by, calm and predictable. It was exactly what Charlotte needed. She'd get up and go to work while Will was still sprawled on the guest bed snoring. She'd come home to find dinner waiting, the place clean and any laundry washed and neatly folded. Well, not as neatly as she would have done it, but she didn't complain. In the evening and into the night they'd work on the stories, still bickering over word choice every once in a while.

Her life felt safe again. Orderly. Three days of counseling a week progressed to one session a week, and then to once every two weeks. Charlotte found herself talking less about the past and her nightmares to Marjorie, and more about the future of her business and her work with Will. She talked about the baby, how he kicked her, how he gave her gas and heartburn and only let her sleep on her right side.

They didn't talk about sex during these sessions. Marjorie made a few half-hearted attempts at discussing it, but Charlotte was still so confused and spooked that they didn't get anywhere. Charlotte had thought casual sex with Will was "bad sex," but in comparison to rape sex, casual sex was pretty wonderful. With Will anyway.

Charlotte felt conflicted because some part of her was developing sexual feelings for Will again. Perhaps it was his kindness and protectiveness, or his handsomeness. Perhaps it was his brains or his dry sense of humor. She didn't care to analyze it, she just understood that her need to connect to him was growing. Maybe it was hormonal, because the bigger her waistline grew, the stronger the pull to reach out to him.

But she didn't want him to know. If anything intimate happened between them, she wanted to be the author of it. She wanted to be the one who initiated it, the one who ceded control. She didn't think she could bear to be coerced, even by subtle flirtation. She couldn't give herself away casually this time. She wasn't sure she could give herself away at all, so she let things ride as she moved into the last trimester of her pregnancy.

Spring came, and her mother's annual Easter dinner, and Charlotte figured it was time to get Will and her parents together again. Before they left, Will called home to wish a happy Easter to his own family, and Charlotte felt an uncomfortable pang of guilt. It was her fault he was stuck here so far away from them. Well, his fault too, but still. She wondered what his family was like. He rarely talked about his home, his parents. She knew he had four sisters, and some nieces and nephews. He spoke to some of them on the phone. Uncle Will this, Uncle Will that. They were young, from the way he talked to them. It was cute and sad at the same time.

"I'm sorry," she said when he hung up.

"Sorry for what?"

"That you miss your family. That you can't be with them today."

He shook his head. "I haven't spent an Easter in London in ages. I haven't been the best son, or brother. Or uncle." His gaze fell on her bump, which was getting too big to camouflage with stylish clothes. She was a whale, and he was having second thoughts. She could see it.

"Being a father will be even harder," she pointed out.

"I'm up for it."

"If you don't want to—"

"Charlotte, let's not hash over this again. Tell me what I need to know to survive this dinner with your parents. Do they still hate me?"

"My mom does, a little," she said. "I told them you were staying at my place, and she doesn't approve of it."

"That's good to know."

"They also don't know the baby's yours. I still haven't told them about our...dalliance...over there. They think you're here because we're working on the stories."

"Our 'dalliance?' What is this, the Canterbury Tales?"

"Would you rather I called it 'living in sin?' That's what my mom calls it."

Will laughed and rubbed his forehead. "Okay. Eventually, you'll have to break the news to them."

"I will, eventually."

And that was that. Charlotte liked that Will was laid back when it came to most matters. It balanced out her tendency to stress.

It also helped in dealing with her folks, because they were barely polite to him at dinner. Borderline rude. Her mother's icy manners embarrassed Charlotte, and she felt vaguely ashamed at the opulence of her parents' house, by the stultifying properness of the dinner service. She couldn't imagine what Will thought of it. He didn't look at her, but kept his gaze trained on his plate through the entire salad course.

Her father made a token stab at conversation when the ham and potatoes came out. "So, how are things in the language business, Mr. Mayfair?"

"It's Dr. Mayfair, daddy," Charlotte said when Will didn't correct him.

"Doctor, is it?" Her father looked back down at his plate, his token attempt at social conversation completed. Will took a sip of wine and glanced at Charlotte.

"Tell them about the dialect," she said. "It's okay. Tell them about the book."

"What book?" Charlotte's mother asked.

"Will and his partner are working on a book about the myths we're translating," said Charlotte. "Not only the myths, but what they might mean to modern people."

Her mother and father made bland, equivocal sounds.

"What I don't understand is why modern people should care about a language that's extinct," her father said.

Charlotte shook her head. "It's not a language book. Or, I guess...it's about more than the language." She gave Will an encouraging look.

He toyed with his silverware, then faced off against her folks. "The most interesting part of my work is the part where anthropology meets words. I research how culture is reflected in language, among other things. The mythologies, the histories, the relationships between languages explain a lot about the history of the people who spoke them."

"And who do you do that for?" her father asked a bit truculently. Her mother slogged wine, nearly spilling it on her dress. "Who does that benefit exactly? Who pays you?"

"Daddy," Charlotte warned under her breath.

"I'm paid by the MacArthur Foundation, a few smaller grants, and my university. I'm affiliated with a university in London."

"Affiliated? Is that a way of saying you teach there?"

Will poked at his potatoes. "I'm not teaching right now."

"So you study these things? Knowledge for the sake of knowledge? I don't see who benefits. No offense, but I've never seen the point of this academia nonsense," her dad said, waving his wineglass and taking a deep drink.

"I guess not many people benefit directly." Will shrugged. "That's probably why I don't make much money at it."

Charlotte couldn't stand it, watching him lie down and take it. She dropped her fork with a clatter. "Money's not the point of what he does. Is it, Will?" Charlotte saw her mother's lips tighten. She didn't care. Will wasn't perfect, but the scope of his life's work didn't deserve to be called nonsense. She turned to her father. "What he does is more important than you realize. It benefits all of humanity. When these languages and histories are gone, they're gone forever. People's thoughts and ideas, gone with no way to get them back—and some of them are wonderful ideas. The stories we uncovered over there are about nature, about the earth. About respect for women, and perseverance and bravery, and love."

Adele twitched. Charlotte knew her mother was a few seconds from bolting the table. Charlotte clamped her mouth shut and felt like bolting too, but then she looked at Will from under her lashes, and he was there again, right there, beneath the self-effacing penitent. The man she knew. The light in his eyes, the half-crooked smile. The secret, speculative intelligence. She hid her own smile behind her napkin as her father blustered out.

"Yes, well, that's very good. I'm a businessman, you know, Mr.—Dr. Mayfair."

"Please, call me Will."

"Yes, anyway, Mayfair. Will. I'll tell ya, I like things in black and white. All these mysteries and histories and foreign language... Do you know how to golf?"

Will answered smoothly, "No, sir."

"Golf's a great game. I don't know that you shouldn't give it a try. What do they play over there in England anyway? Soccer?"

"They call it football, Gordon," her mother said. Charlotte stifled laughter but Will nodded with a perfectly straight face.

"That's right, Mrs. Rowe. But I've never been one for competitive sports. I enjoy swimming."

"Swimming," Charlotte's father repeated, unable to come up with anything polite to say about that.

By the time they were done with dinner, Charlotte's nerves were frazzled, but no one had come to blows. It felt like success, and a little bit of healing on her parents' part. Maybe the man living with their daughter wasn't a soul-dead monster. Imagine that. After dinner, her dad even invited Will to the garage to look at his collection of vintage Cadillacs. Charlotte prayed Will knew something about car engines and hoped for the best. Her mother wasn't nearly as relaxed. She said something about pruning her rose bushes and slipped out the back. Her mother's pride, those rosebushes—just as Charlotte had been, once upon a time.

Charlotte followed a few moments later. It was a cool evening for April, and a breeze blew her hair as she walked across the yard. Waddled really. God, she was getting big. It was time to have this conversation, whether her mother wanted to or not.

"Hi, Mama," she said when she reached the rose garden.

Her mother looked up and brushed an errant wisp of hair from her face. "Charlotte, dear me. Why aren't you inside putting your feet up? Did you enjoy dinner?"

"I enjoyed the parts of it when you two weren't ganging up on Will."

Her mother sniffed and went back to work, snipping off branches with crisp efficiency and placing them in a neat pile. "We did nothing of the sort. It was nice to see your friend again. When is he going home?"

Your friend. She wouldn't make this easy. Adele Rowe never made anything easy. Charlotte shrugged and bent down to help her mother slip a sheaf of branches into a lawn bag. "I don't know. Probably after daddy's done showing off his cars."

"I mean, when is he heading home to London? Doesn't he live there?"

"Yes, but...I don't know. I don't know when he's going home."

A tense silence descended. Charlotte looked at her mother and took a deep breath.

"Mama, while we were over in Adygea, we developed a pretty close relationship. Me and Will."

Her mother made an impatient sound. "I'm not completely naive, Charlotte. I know you think I am."

"Anyway, he took a paternity test, and it turns out this baby...it's his. His and mine."

Even as she said it she could feel her mother's spirit breaking. In generations upon generations of her mother's proper southern family, she doubted anyone had ever required something so vile as a paternity test. Adele went back to pruning. *Clip. Clip. Clip.*

"Mama, did you hear me?"

She snapped the shears harder. "Lord deliver me. Yes, I heard you. Grandma Margaret must be turning over in her grave." She stopped and glared at Charlotte. "You know, we tried so hard to raise you right. To give you everything, but not spoil you. To raise you with a level head on your shoulders."

"I do have a level head on my shoulders."

"Like hell you do." Charlotte blanched. In thirty years of her life, she'd never heard her mother use the word *hell*. She kicked at the ground, feeling like a shamed child.

"I thought you'd be happy. It's good news."

"Good news? That it's his, and not one of the savages who raped my poor daughter half a world away while I sat here and worried for you, and cried myself to sleep? For months, Charlotte. I cried for months." Her mother broke off, covering her mouth, collecting herself. Charlotte hated the way her mother refused to cry. "Good news?" she went on. "That you're pregnant by this man you're not married to? That you've known since, when? Last summer? He's not even American."

"What does that have to do with anything?"

"Does he have any intention to marry you? To support the baby? Will he expect you to leave Savannah?"

"God forbid I would leave Savannah."

"Yes, God forbid it. Look what happened last time you left." Her mother did cry then, her face crumpling into tears. Charlotte stood across from her, an eviscerated rose bush between them. "And your business is here, Charlotte. Everything you worked for. How could you throw everything away for that—that man?"

The bewilderment in her voice was too much, and Charlotte started to cry too. "I haven't thrown anything away. It just happened. This all just happened to me."

"No. You left! You wanted adventure, you were bored. I warned you. I asked you not to go. Was it worth it, for those godforsaken stories? I don't care who they benefit. The price was too high." She brushed away tears, taking up her clippers again. "What happened to my little baby? My little Charlotte running through the roses? I miss her, I really do. Where did she go?"

She went to the edge of the earth. She was seeking the meaning of life. Charlotte started to turn away, to retreat. Her mother's broken voice stopped her.

"You'll run off to London, I know you will. My only daughter, with my only grandchild."

"Grandson! Mama, it's a boy. Our boy, mine and Will's. Can't you pretend to be happy for us?"

"You'll be all alone over there, a new mama, with *him*."

Charlotte's hands curled into fists. "You can say his name. It's Will. You act like he's some criminal, like he's dangerous."

"He is. I don't understand how you don't see that, after everything, *everything* that's happened to you because of him."

"It wasn't his fault. You don't understand."

"No, I don't. I don't understand at all."

They both fell silent again. The only sound was the sniffles and snuffles of two southern women trying to be dignified while they cried. She walked back to her mother with heavy steps and reached out for her. They hugged and cried a little more, wetting each other's cheeks. "I know you don't understand," Charlotte said. "But you have to trust me. He's a good man." She pulled away and looked down at the ground, at the cut-back rose bush. Her mother had really done a number on it. "Can you tell Daddy about Will and the baby? You would know the best way to do it. I just can't."

Her mother shrugged, wiping away the last of her tears. "Oh, your father will take it all right. He seems to think that man is in love with you."

"Will didn't have to come here. He didn't have to come to Savannah, or to Easter dinner to face you and Daddy. I tried to send him away when he first got here, months ago, but he wouldn't go."

Her mother sighed. "Do you love him, at least? Was it all worth it? I hope so."

"Oh, Mama," she said softly. "I hope so too. But I don't know yet. I'm just trying to make the best of what happened. I can't change it, I can't make it go away. You have to forgive me and Will, because we can't go back and do anything differently now."

"I know." Her mother stroked her cheek, a rare show of maternal affection. "I know that, and I forgive you, but you'll have to let me be sad for what might have been, just for a little while. I'll get over it, I promise. I just need time."

Charlotte understood that. She smiled at her mother. "A few weeks is all you get, because I don't want my baby to have a sad grandma."

Her mother chuckled at that. "A sad grandma. God forbid." She rolled her eyes and picked up her shears again. "Being a grandma—period—is bad enough."

* * * * *

Will and Charlotte went home soon afterward, with a gallon of sweet tea nestled beside Will's feet on the passenger side of Charlotte's sedan. "It was supposed to be for dinner," she explained, "but they cracked out the wine instead."

"They needed fortification because I was coming."

"No. Well, maybe." They both laughed. "Actually, I think my mom and dad have made peace with you, in their usual passive-aggressive way. I'm sorry it was uncomfortable."

"It was horrible."

"I know, but I think it really helped."

"And you got some sweet tea out of it."

"Yes, and that."

She waited for the mocking, the teasing. Talking about sweet tea took her back to that clearing by the cabin. To the lake, to the ring of mountains. To warm, weak tea with no ice, and his spit-take off the porch. She waited, but no mockery came.

At home, Will stuck the sweet tea in the fridge while Charlotte laid out the notebooks and index cards and booted up their laptops. They worked for a while on yet another segment of Lepsch's adventures, the reckless warrior still looking for the edge of the earth. Charlotte had to hand it to Lepsch, he never gave up.

"Can I have some of that sweet tea?" Will asked, interrupting her thoughts. "With the ice and everything?"

She paused over her notes. "You won't like it."

"I've never had the real deal, have I? So how can you know if I'll like it or not?"

"Honestly, Will. You don't have to drink it on my account."

"I see. You don't want to share. That's fine."

She rolled her eyes. "You won't like it, and then you'll start giving me the business—"

"Business? What is this 'business' you speak of?"

"And if you spit it out on my carpet, I'll kill you. I'll literally kill you dead."

"So violent, Charlotte." He sighed. "Never mind. I'm not thirsty anymore. Not that thirsty anyway," he added under his breath.

Charlotte stood and pushed back her chair. "Fine. I'll get you some."

"You don't have to," he murmured.

"Oh, you're drinking it," she said on her way to the kitchen. "You're not backing out now."

She got some glasses and started filling them with ice while he bent back over the book. She stole a glance at him, her own reckless warrior who wouldn't give up. Why did he have to look so handsome and serious when they worked? Why did he make her want him when she was so scared of feeling that way? She closed the freezer door and stopped still, staring at it. In a perfect line in the middle, he'd made a sentence.

I SEE YOU WELL

She ripped open the refrigerator and pulled out the tea, splashing it into the glasses. *I see you well. I see you well.* She carried them over with her heart banging in her chest. She placed one at his side and he smiled up at her, just a glance.

"Thanks, Charlotte."

Chaaar-lit. He took a sip and she watched. He didn't like it. She could see the grimace he restrained. He took a second sip and nodded.

"You know, it's not so bad. I like it more now, drunk properly with ice. Thank you." He took yet another sip, choked it down, really.

Charlotte stared at him, and all her thoughts converged into one simple understanding. *You hate it, and you're drinking it anyway to make me happy.*

I see you well. I see you, Will.

She reached for him, touched his hair, that shock of white blond hair, then spread her fingers on his cheek. "I know you don't like it."

"I love it," he insisted.

"I saw what you wrote."

He glanced at his computer screen, then realized what she was talking about. "Oh." His hand came over hers. "It's true, you know."

"I know." Her breath caught in her chest. "No one has ever seen me like you."

Will stood and pulled her close. They shared a shuddering embrace, as close an embrace as her belly would allow. She kissed him, or perhaps he kissed her. Someone kissed someone and then she was grasping his shoulders and touching his fine blond hair again. Time slowed down so she felt every sensation and heard every sound. The scrape of his chair as she leaned against it, her moans and whimpers as he enfolded her in his arms. "I love you, Will," she whispered against his ear. "I should have told you before now."

He pressed his cheek to hers. "I've loved you forever. But I'm not good enough for you. I'm not."

She clutched at him. "You're perfect for me."

He kissed her neck, held her and caressed her from her earlobe to the curve of her shoulder. It was intoxicating to feel this side of him again, his desire, his intensity. She was dizzy with wanting him, all her fears chased away by the comfort of his touch. "Will..." It was a plea, an appeal to connect now before she lost her nerve.

He studied her face, then took her hand and led her to her bedroom. She wanted to push him back on the bed and straddle him, but he fretted about her belly and helped her lie down like she was made of glass. She indulged his protectiveness, then turned and gracelessly batted all her pillows out of the way.

She turned back as he sprawled out beside her, stroking all over her with warm, firm hands. She waited for fear to come, or disgust, but all she felt was a need that cried out for him. She pulled at his clothes, felt the hard outline of his cock against her hand.

He drew away. "What if I hurt you? Or hurt the baby?"

"No, he's cushioned. You won't hurt him."

Will shed his clothes, slowly, watching her the whole time, and undressed her too, cupping her heavy breasts with reverent hands, and caressing the mound of her baby bump. "Are you sure I won't hurt you?"

She knew he was talking about more than the baby. He searched her face, perhaps looking for that disgust and fear she'd expected to feel. She caught his gaze and held it. "I need you to take me like you used to. When it was just you and me and nothing else in the world. Do you remember?"

"Oh, God." His words were half-moan, half-sigh. "I can't wait to be inside you again." He slid his fingers to her center, into the wet warmth of her desire. There was no numbness, no pain, just the shivery thrill of arousal she remembered from so long ago. She parted her thighs, arching toward him for more of his touch.

"Yes, open for me," he whispered. "That's right. Lovely Charlotte. I never could resist you." His fingers slipped inside as he licked her nipples and bit the tender skin around them. She felt a melting, delicious anticipation flow through her veins.

"Will. Oh, that feels good." She wanted him so badly, felt a nagging emptiness where she wanted him to be. His cock rested on her leg, hard and torrid against her skin. She massaged his rigid length and ran the pad of her thumb over the tip. A drop of pre-cum slid across the head beneath her finger. "First... Can I...?" she stammered. "I want to..."

He released her with a question in his gaze, and she slid down and took his cock in her hands, re-familiarizing herself with its velvety surface and the rough texture of his balls. She needed to do this, to know it was him and no other. To know she could control him and hold him back until she was ready to give in. He groaned softly as she traced his shaft, exploring every contour. It was Will's scent, Will's shape and size. Will's fingers twisting in her hair, encouraging her. She leaned to lick and kiss around the swollen head. His cock bucked against her lips. "God, Charlotte. Don't...not too long..."

She opened her mouth and took him inside. His hands tightened in her hair in a spasmodic grasp, and his groan sounded like pleading. He let her control the depth of his thrust, let her taste and caress him however she liked. Another drop of pre-cum created a salty tang in her mouth. He made a hissing sound.

"Enough." He nudged her away and turned her so she was on her side, her back pressed against the front of him. It was the only practical position in her advanced state of pregnancy. His hands settled over her breasts and his hips shifted until they were aligned with hers, the head of his cock poised just at her entrance. Then he paused, and they both seemed to realize at the same time that no condom would be needed now.

"Love me, Will. Please."

He laid his head beside hers and moved into her, stretching her, filling her. His scratchy chest hair scraped against her back and his legs cradled hers, lifting her with each thrust. It didn't feel frightening or bad. It felt safe. She gasped, so content to once again be possessed by him. He stopped, looking down at her in concern.

"Am I hurting you?"

"No," she finally managed to get out. "No, but—" She reached back and grasped at him. He slid out and in again, smooth as silk. "Hold me so close. Please hold me. I don't want you to let me go."

He turned her head and kissed her hard, at the same time trapping her hands against her chest. Against her heart, above the place their baby curled and rested. "I'm not going anywhere, and I'm not letting you go." His fingers curled around hers, holding them tight. He made love to her with care, not crushing her but not releasing her either. Hot arousal flared in her pussy, building to a heavy throb between her legs. He reached down with one hand and found her clit, teasing the bud in a maddening rhythm. She shot toward climax, the helplessly wild, uncontrolled orgasm only he could give her. He gave her so much more though. Her humanness, her sexuality. Her freely-given consent. Her legs clenched as he drove faster with his hips.

"I'm going to come," she gasped. She jerked with each skillful touch of his fingers.

"Wait for me."

"I can't. It feels too wonderful."

His teeth closed on her shoulder while his hands traveled down and grabbed her hips. Her climax came over her in waves, shooting out from her pussy to her thighs and her huge belly. She could feel her womb contract, a rolling, exquisite fruition. The release was so profound, almost apocalyptic. He shuddered behind her, holding her hips through the tumult of his rough, culminating thrusts. She wanted his roughness, his total surrender. Her surrender also. *I give up. I need you. This has to work, because we belong together.* He collapsed against her, his heartbeat deep and steady against her back. He was still grasping her hands. He nuzzled against her and made some light, contented sound.

It was a wonderful sound, saying much more than words. Language had brought them together, and then had seemed to come between them. But it wasn't language they needed. Language wasn't dependable. Sometimes languages just disappeared. But this...this...

She shivered as he ran a hand up her back. He let her pull away and turn to face him. They lay together, silent, exploring one another with mouths and fingertips. Then she said, "There's this language called Ubykh."

Will smiled at her. "Stop. You'll make me cry." He leaned back and stroked a finger down her nose, across her cheek. "I love you so. I fell for you the second I saw you. There was something about you."

She laughed. "You're a liar. A romantic liar, but still."

"No, it's true. The look on your face when you got off that plane in Maykop... The utter need to break down, and that stubborn refusal to let it show. Oh, Charlotte. You're a hundred times braver than me. A million times stronger. You've taught me about real bravery, not just the warrior stuff from the stories." He grinned at her. "And you've taught me to not be a super judgmental idiot."

She laughed, remembering that long ago conversation, even as tears gathered in her eyes. She peeked up at him with a wobbly frown. "You're still an idiot, anyway."

"Well." He pulled her close and kissed her, right over her brimming eyelids. "I'm not as much an idiot as I was."

Chapter Sixteen: Wheel

They stayed in her bed the entire next day, only stumbling to the kitchen a few times for some food and sweet tea. Will needed the sugar for stamina, and downed the cloying beverage with a suddenly unquenchable thirst. He thirsted for her too, her skin, her scent, her welcoming wetness. Between making love to her, they talked and laughed and made shy, tentative plans for a future together. He felt almost painfully close to her, even when she wasn't in his arms.

He realized now there had never been any question of leaving her. There wasn't the slightest possibility of them living apart. He told her so before they drifted to sleep in her silly ruffled bed.

He dreamed of her all night, the sound of her, the smell of her, and slept late the following morning. When his eyes fluttered open, she was standing beside the bed watching him. She wore one of his shirts over the round loveliness of her belly, which made something primal and male puff up inside him. She'd styled her hair in a quick, messy twist that was cute but awfully un-Charlotte-like. He reached out for her. "Everything okay?"

"I'm fine. But you look wrecked."

He stretched and moved over, drawing her down beside him. "It's the first time I've slept peacefully in forever," he said. "How are you?"

"I've been on the phone with my mother. So, I've been better."

"Oh, no." He traced over her forehead and across her cheek. "What did you talk about?"

"You, a little. She called to apologize about Easter. About being 'unpleasant' to you, and freaking out in the rose garden and crying in front of me, which is a huge crime in her eyes."

"She's not handling the idea of you and me very well, is she?"

"I don't know." Her eyes closed as he slid his fingertips across her skin. "She wasn't exactly ecstatic, but she wasn't shocked either. I think she suspected all along."

"Will she boycott the wedding, do you think?"

Charlotte's eyes popped open. "Is that a proposal? Because if it is, it's a pretty shoddy one."

Will sighed and kissed her, lingering over her lips. "I don't seem to go about anything the right way." He gazed down at her, drinking in the beauty of her exotic light-hazel eyes, her tousled, mussed-up hair. "Charlotte, I adore you," he said ardently. "Will you marry me?"

"I might." She cut her eyes at him and rolled away, onto her side. "I'm going to have to think about it. I mean, if I marry an Englishman—excuse me, a *Briton*—I'll have to learn to drive on the wrong side of the road and all that."

"If I can learn to stomach sweet tea, you can learn to drive, sugar."

She laughed as he pulled her back against him. He rested his hand on her belly.

"We don't have to live in England," he said. "I can work anywhere. Even Savannah, I expect. Maybe I can be your assistant home organizer."

"Oh Lord, no." She shook her head and put a hand over his. "The language world needs you. I wouldn't be averse to leaving Savannah though. Going somewhere new. Not quite as far as Adygea, but far enough away that we don't have to have dinner with my parents very often."

"I'm one hundred percent behind that idea." He was quiet a moment. "We could go anywhere we'd both be happy. Any place we thought might be a good place to raise a child, and live happily ever after."

Happily ever after. He'd never been much of one for fairy tales, but he was willing to chase happily ever after with Charlotte all the way to the ends of the earth. She was having her usual effect on his senses. His groin tightened in response to her closeness. He shifted his hips away from her so she wouldn't feel his cock rising like a flag against her ass. She chuckled, not fooled for a second.

He shook his head against her hair. "I'm sorry. I can't resist you."

"You don't have to resist me."

"Part of me still expects you to get angry afterward and tell me to stop seducing you."

"I think it's a little late for that now."

He slid a hand up her side and cupped one of her breasts, then brushed the pad of his thumb over her nipple, basking in her tiny shiver. "Are you saying it's okay to seduce you? Say, for instance, right now?"

She wiggled back against him with a sigh. "I wonder why you never gave up. Before. Why didn't you just give up when I always freaked out afterward?"

He eased down her stretchy maternity leggings. "I can be really tenacious when it comes to some things." His fingers delved beneath her panties.

"Tenacious," Charlotte breathed. "That's a great word."

"I know better ones." He deftly inched down her panties and threw them aside. "Intrepid. Adamant." He pulled off her top with a flourish. "Persevering."

"Diligent?" she offered as he did away with her bra.

"Diligent is nice, but perhaps a little too tame for the way I feel around you." He sucked in a breath as she pressed back against his cock.

"Intransigent then. Unrelenting."

Vixen. She knew the big, juicy words undid him. He bit down on her earlobe. "Oh God, fuck yes."

He seated himself in her from behind. Oh, how it felt to be inside her. Her pussy clenched around him, making his balls tighten with mind-numbing pleasure. She moaned and reached back to grasp his thighs. He loved the way she turned to pure animal longing in his arms. He stopped her, taking her hands in his.

"No need to draw blood," he whispered. "Just let me make love to my future wife." He pressed deeper inside her. *I see you so, so well, my Circassian love. My lens, worth an untold fortune.* "Does that feel good?" he asked, for no other reason than to hear her voice.

"Oh, Will." *Oh, wheel.*

He gave a triumphant laugh and thrilled to the feel of her squirming back against him. He stroked her clit as he drove in and out of her, teasing the slick bud to hear her beg for more. Beg for it harder, then softer, until her voice dissolved into incoherent moans of ecstasy. His own arousal resonated and peaked, a shuddering pressure in his middle that rolled hot and wide across every part of him when his orgasm arrived. He buried himself in her and knew true completion when she contracted around him, gasping out her release. It was an elemental joining, a communion, as always. He didn't question it or marvel at it anymore—with them, it just *was*. She turned to him and wrapped her arms around his neck, and he splayed his hand on her back to hold her against him.

He reached up and wound his fingers in her hair, her long, thick locks. He tilted her head back and kissed her endlessly, for all the prayers answered by those soft delicious lips. Between them, her beautiful bump and the mystery of their future nestled and grew. Another heart beating. Little hands curling and feet kicking and eyes waiting to see something beautiful. Ears waiting to hear all the wonders of the world. Will knew they would teach the baby her grandfather's dialect, if he didn't already carry it like some secret code woven into the synapses of his brain. Why not prevent something worthwhile from dying? So many words, meaning so many things to so many people. Words and people and meaning and centuries and centuries...

But now, no words at all, just her kiss and the scent of her skin.

* * * * *

They married a few weeks later in her parents' rose garden. It was a small, intimate affair, not only because it was planned quickly, but because Charlotte was big as a house and moved about as gracefully as one. This definitely wasn't how she'd pictured her wedding, but it was still perfect to her. They danced and dined, they celebrated and made toasts to a future that wasn't uncertain anymore. Roger came with his partner Perry, and her parents invited several of Charlotte's oldest, dearest friends. Will's parents and a couple of his sisters made the trip over the ocean, while the others sent gifts and effusive cards of congratulation. Her mother played hostess with a smile, despite the unconventionality of the proceedings. She even finally—grudgingly—began to address her new son-in-law as Will rather than "that man."

After the ceremony, as the guests sat and relaxed in the garden, a new arrival showed up. Ivo charged across the lawn with an energy belied by his age. Charlotte and Will had made peace with Ivo over his part in endangering her, because without Ivo's good-natured tampering, they never would have met. The old scholar held out his hands to Charlotte, then drew back to take in her voluminous white dress.

"My dear, you are the most beautiful bride to exist. I swear this."

Will came over to shake his hand. "You missed the ceremony, old man."

"I have been traveling. I thought I set my clocks correctly but I am two hours off," Ivo said with a rueful grin. "I am late, but I am here. I come to give congratulations to a very special couple."

Will tsked at his old friend. "Yes, and to see how we're getting along with the stories, I suppose."

Ivo clasped his hands, suppressing a smile. "The stories. Yes, perhaps."

Since a honeymoon was out of the question, they ended up at Charlotte's place later that evening sharing the newest stories with Ivo, who made a blissfully clueless wedding-night third wheel.

"Ah," he sighed, touching the mildewed cover lightly. "Lucky book. Rescued. Such beautiful stories you have brought us, Charlotte, as well as this book itself."

"Will brought the book," she said. "I never would have had the nerve to steal it."

"I didn't steal it," Will protested. "I plan to give it back."

"You must take care, you know." The old man frowned. "The humidity here will damage the parchment."

"I'll put it into storage soon. Until it can be returned safely."

A shadow crossed Ivo's face. "They still fight. Is very bad."

Charlotte hadn't known. Sometimes she reminisced about the cabin in the clearing and the beautiful mountains, but she tried not to think about the tragic aspects of the place they'd left, the battling factions of the region. She didn't look for the Russian republics in the news and never heard anything about them in passing. The rest of the world seemed happy to remain oblivious. Like her.

But Will followed the news of the area. She could tell from the look on his face. "They'll fight until they destroy everything, or run out of money. Nothing will be solved, for all that."

"I agree," said Ivo. "Terrible, how they fight over meaningless things. In a way, war is a failure of language. Of communication."

"Not always." Charlotte gave Will a pointed look. "Sometimes the opposing sides can't agree on what they want."

"Or they claim they want one thing, when they really want something else," he shot back.

"Yes, it is so." Ivo nodded, out of the loop as usual. "It is unfortunate. When we cease to communicate, we cease to be human."

"My grandfather used to say language was the heart of humanity," Charlotte said.

Ivo turned to her, fist upraised. "Yes. I would have liked this man, your grandfather. I share his view. That is why the work we do is so important. And this..." He indicated the aged text. "This did end up being an important artifact after all." He turned to Charlotte. "You will finish the translation and help us write the stories into a book? But I know, you have important things to do. Being mama and wife. This will take your attention. I understand."

Charlotte smiled. "I'll finish, don't worry. Although Will could probably do it now. Or you, if you looked at his notes on the language."

"No, it must be you," Ivo insisted. "The story is your voice so far. Is best to be your voice until the end. The translation must be unbroken. Because you see..." He looked at her tenderly. "Only you can tell the story in your particular way."

She glanced at Will and he nodded. "It's true. It's better if you tell the whole story. Scholars will recognize a change in narrator. You've done a great job so far."

"A great job!" Ivo echoed enthusiastically. "Is gripping, your story. But I will wait for the ending. I am a patient man."

Charlotte put a hand to her waist. There it was again. An unmistakable tightening. She'd been having random, mild contractions since the morning, but this one had a harder edge.

"You might have to wait a little while longer, Ivo. I think I'm in labor." She bent down, grimacing. "Yeah. I'm pretty sure."

* * * * *

By the time they got to the hospital, Charlotte was panicking. This was not at all what she'd expected and planned for. It was not an organized process. It was messier, faster, slimier, scarier than she could have imagined. The labor pains increased to a terrifying intensity, and then grew worse still.

Will leaned over her hospital bed, stroking her hair and speaking to her in a calming voice. "Charlotte, listen to me. I want you to be in so much pain. I want this labor to be awful for you, unbearable."

The OB nurse gaped at Will. He smiled back. "It's a Caucasus language thing, you see. You tell someone the opposite of what you actually—well—" The nurse's eyes widened another degree. "It's kind of hard to explain. *Ooof.*"

His breath came out in a whoosh as Charlotte's foot connected with his stomach. "I will mess you up, Will Mayfair," she groaned. "Don't start with your fucking language—stupid—idiotic— I'm in fucking labor. Oh my God!"

She tensed as another contraction shook her. This wasn't how it was supposed to be. She was cursing, screeching, and humiliatingly, vomiting. She had envisioned a calm, placid birth experience, an epidural to numb any pain and Will smiling proudly at her bedside as she breezed into the miracle of motherhood. She'd wanted to give birth gracefully, damn it. She aimed another random kick at Will's solar plexus.

"Gently, darling," he said.

"I swear to holy—Will, if you don't make this stop— You're just fucking standing there!"

"My word," came a familiar voice from the door. "Even in labor, ladies do not use such language."

The harried nurse held Charlotte back as she swiped for her mother's windpipe. "Okay. Breathe through it," the nurse ordered. "And you two"—she tossed a look at Will and her mother—"Either pipe down or get out."

"I need pain medication," wailed Charlotte, grabbing the nurse by her teddy-bear printed scrubs. She wanted to kill those teddy bears. "I can't take this. I can't. Give me some drugs."

"We don't have time. The doctor's on his way." The nurse signaled another nurse in the hallway. "The baby's not going to wait for the anesthesiologist."

"I'll hold it in until he gets here," Charlotte moaned.

"Yes, hold it in," said Charlotte's mother, as the long suffering nurse rolled her eyes. "Until after midnight, please. I can't bear the idea of celebrating my daughter's wedding anniversary and my grandchild's birthday on the same day every year. Just imagine—the announcements in the newspaper side by side." She shuddered at the thought of it.

The nurse pointed a finger at her. "I suggest silence."

Charlotte burst into tears, reaching for her mother as a strangling contraction petered out, leaving her a wrung-out mess. She knew another one was coming right on its heels. "Mama, this hurts so bad. Help me." She turned her face into Will's shoulder as he cradled her. "I'm so scared. I can't bear this. I'm going to die from this."

"You won't." Will rubbed her lower back, the spot that wrenched and spasmed each time a new contraction came. "You won't die. You're so strong."

Her mother fed her ice chips and held her hand. "I know you think you won't survive. I remember, Charlotte. I thought you would crack me in two, but as soon as I saw you, you were my heart. My very own heart."

Charlotte could barely fathom her mother's words, or the tender expression on her face. The nurse was snapping orders to Will. They hauled back her legs and the nurse said words that made no sense to her. "Bear down."

Charlotte gawked.

"When the contraction comes," the nurse explained patiently. "Bear down when you feel the contraction start."

Charlotte had no idea what she meant...until the bands tightened around her middle again with excruciating power. She started to panic, but her body responded to some deeper impulse and she felt the need to push. "Push down low," the nurse said. "Push as hard as you can. Let's get this baby born."

"But wait until after midnight if you can," her mother pleaded.

Charlotte shrieked and pushed and braced and pushed and kicked and pushed. It was a relief to push, but the pain didn't lessen. At last her doctor arrived and took over.

"Okay, now. We're almost there. Are you ready? Isn't this exciting?"

He smiled at her, a kindly silver-haired physician. Will put a restraining hand around her ankle before she could give the man the kick in the groin he deserved.

"Gently," he whispered again. "Our baby's almost here."

"Go fuck yourself," she whispered back. Another contraction and burning, burning pain. A ring of fire that felt like a vortex pulling her under while simultaneously tearing her apart. "No, no, no, no, no," Charlotte yelled.

"Yes, yes, yes," the doctor said. "That's it!"

A few minutes before midnight, the arrival of a healthy baby boy turned a wedding day into a birthday. Her mother griped, but Will and Charlotte could only cradle their baby and stare.

"You did it," Will said. "God, Charlotte. Just look at him."

The screaming newborn had a fuzz of white blond hair like his father, and clocked in at a healthy seven-and-a-half pounds. Charlotte adored him from the second she saw him, adored everything about him. His newborn smell, his shrill screams, his mottled face. As soon as he calmed down enough to open his eyes, Charlotte thought the blue was like the color of the skies over the mountains. "Wow. I can barely believe you're here," she whispered against his warm baby skin. "I've been waiting forever to meet you, beautiful boy."

Chapter Seventeen: This

They named him William Radcliffe Simon Mayfair Jr.

Will thought it a bit narcissistic to force his own unwieldy name on his offspring, but Charlotte and her mother stood firm. It was a southern thing, apparently. Will had jokingly suggested Lepsch, only to be smacked upside the head by Charlotte. Charlotte's mother left the hospital in ecstasy to order some blankets for her new grandson, muttering about four initials and monograms. Soon after, his parents and sisters arrived, along with Charlotte's father, who hung around in his usual silent but attentive way. Family was everywhere, smiling and celebrating.

Will held his son and thought that Charlotte's grandfather was wrong. Language wasn't the heart of humanity. His son was.

From the very start, they both loved their son to distraction. They called him Junior at first because he was so tiny and adorable. At his two week checkup, he was still Junior, and Will had a feeling even if he grew as big as his father, he'd be dogged by the diminutive label. *Call him Junior, and he'll grow up big and strong.*

Will officially left his university post in London, resigned his MacArthur grant, and became, for the first time in his life, a kept man. Charlotte's business was thriving, each new branch a success. Thank goodness for all the disorganization in the world. It allowed him to stay home and play daddy to Junior, while embarking on his own independent language studies whenever the baby and Charlotte didn't need him. By the time Junior was two months old, things had calmed considerably. Charlotte went back to work part time, but saved plenty of hours to spend with Junior, and with Will, as they slowly worked their way to the end of the Circassian text.

But it was plodding progress, because they usually found other things to do with their time when Junior napped. Many varied and carnal things.

"Oh, Will, yes, yes! Right there!"

Will chuckled and pressed his hand over her mouth. "Shh. He'll hear."

"I don't care," she gasped against his palm. "We'll have to...*ahhh, yes, yes, yes.*" She sucked in a breath. "We'll have to soundproof the room."

He thrust into her again, moving his hips in the particular cadence he knew drove her wild. "Yes, we'll have to if my wife can't find a way to moan a bit more softly."

"Your fault," she said. She ground her hips against him as he quickened his pace. As always, the wildness found them, the same wildness that had pulled them together from the moment they'd met and walked to Will's SUV at the airport. The wildness came wherever, whenever they were together. She clenched him as her body shook in surrender. His own orgasm sparked and fired forth. He was the one then who had to clamp his lips together. He buried his face against her neck and whispered words rather than shouted them. "Charlotte, I love you. Jesus, baby, I see you really well right now."

She always laughed when he said that, and pulled his head back and covered his face with kisses. He never complained, and he didn't complain now.

They showered together when they managed to roll out of bed. It amused him that she still loved her showers so much. He thought she probably just appreciated them more now.

He appreciated them too. He loved to run his fingers over her changed body, explore the novel curves and textures of motherhood. He loved the potent fullness of her breasts. He loved the way the water streamed over her skin, following nature's hills and valleys, collecting in the hollow of her clavicle for him to lick and kiss.

"I thirst for you," he declared passionately. He could have said it in two dozen languages but the easiest way to say it was to take her again.

Still later, she spread her notebooks on the bed and pored over them while he brushed her wet hair. When he pulled a tangle, she groused, but she was otherwise quite absorbed. They'd come to the last couple pages. The very end. It was an enormous moment, one they couldn't bear to put off even though Junior was due to wake soon. She read her notes to him as she wrote them.

"Lepsch the warrior traveled until his shoes wore down to his toes, and his walking stick grew shorter than a span. Vast distances he crossed, but he never arrived at the edge of the earth. Defeated, he returned to the Tree Goddess, his feet heavy, his heart..." She paused. "I don't know... *ma' she*."

"Broken?"

"Debilitated."

He put the brush down and squeezed her from behind. "These big words, my God. I can't be held liable for what happens."

She pushed him back, laughing. "Stop it. Focus." She shifted her notes back to rights and kept reading. "She held him as he wept." Charlotte stopped again. "Wept. Do you think that means they had sex again?"

"I think this time he probably really wept. What's the word?"

"Wept. *Vehnzhe*."

"Hmm..." He thought on it a moment, before becoming distracted by the curve of her neck. Charlotte read on as he pushed aside her hair to press kisses against her nape.

"She held him as he wept. She soothed him and said, 'What did you learn on your travels?' He told her, 'I have learned that the earth has no edge. I have learned that the human body is harder than the hardest steel. I have learned that the most difficult road is the one traveled alone.'"

Will was nibbling her ear now, the hairbrush forgotten. She turned to kiss him before returning to her notes. "'Don't you see?' chided the Tree Goddess. 'If you had stayed, you would have found what you needed right here, with me.' With these words, she placed in his arms their child, a baby sun."

Will, only half-listening, stopped in surprise. "A son?"

"No, a sun. Like in the sky. *Se'tere.* Sun and son sound alike in English but they're totally different words in the dialect."

Will mulled it over for a moment. "So he knocked her up with a big sunshine, did he?"

Charlotte went back to the notes again. "'This is our child,' she told him. 'Guard him well. By the light of this sun, you will never be lost.'"

Will stroked his fingers down the waterfall of her hair, made even thicker by motherhood. "They made love for seven days and made a baby that was the sun."

"A creation story," she breathed.

Will nodded against her shoulder. "Creation stories are common in mythology. I rather liked this one. Although you and I only took one night to make our son." His fingers trailed down to rub her now-flat waistline.

"Yes, one very lucky night."

He looked at her notes. "Is that it? The end?"

She turned the page, scanning the remaining text. "No, that's not the end. But the end is too sad."

"What do you mean, it's too sad? What happens?"

"The warrior loses the sun. The baby sun wanders off and is never found and"—she flipped a page back and forth, double-checking—"Lepsch and his people live forever lost, flailing around in misery and grief."

Will cursed softly but viciously in Adyghe. "After all that, that's how it ends?"

She closed the text with a sigh. "I'm afraid so. I can hardly believe it."

He grimaced in mock despair. "How are we supposed to make the bestseller list with this kind of crap to work with?"

"I guess mythology isn't known for its happy endings."

Will laid back, pulling her with him. "Mm. I don't know. We could all use a cautionary tale. Let's be sure that doesn't happen to us. I've been lost and flailing long enough."

She smiled, stroking his hair. "I'm sure that ending was more of their reverse-psychology magic. You know what I think? Life is what you make of it."

"I think so too."

"Will you be my sunshine, and shine on me?" she whispered. "So I don't get lost?"

He grinned at her. "I'd rather be your warrior." He pressed against her, his spear at the ready. "I feel a crying jag coming on. A big one."

She laughed, a wonderful ecstatic sound, but then she sobered. "You can be my warrior, but you can't leave me to go on any quests."

"No, no quests for me. I've already been to the edge of the earth, remember?" He kissed her nose and her parted lips. "That's where I found you."

From two doors down, a demanding wail disrupted their intimate moment. Will groaned against her cheek. "Son's up. Or sun. Whatever you please, but he sounds awfully hungry."

"You go get him while I clear the notebooks away."

Will stood and walked down the hall to the nursery. Afternoon light fell across the room onto the mural they'd painted on the wall. A smiling celestial sun, with undulating rays and an impish twinkle in its eyes. *I'll be damned*, Will thought.

He turned away to pick up Junior and held the baby to his body, soothing and calming him. He performed a quick nappy swap at the ruthlessly organized changing table. So many bins. His wife went on sometimes about "the power of the bin," which rather disturbed him, but Will would take the good with the bad.

"Are you ready to go see your mama?" he asked his son in Charlotte's own language. "She's waiting for you."

Charlotte stretched on the bed, smiling as they entered. Junior was furious by now, kicking his chubby arms and legs, demanding what he knew his mother could give him. Will handed him over and she held the baby close, offering him her breast. His son wasted no time latching on and sucking. Will felt faintly jealous but much more impressed with the sweetness of it all. Charlotte laid back, relaxed, her eyes fluttering closed.

Will lay beside them, watching Junior's fat little hand reach out and clutch Charlotte's hair before relaxing into a half-open fist. One tiny finger found a curl and twisted it absently, around and around and around as he drank.

Will stared at that little finger working Charlotte's hair into a tight coil like some turning helix. A turning planet, with Charlotte and Will's feet like roots in the earth, and their infant's eyes reflecting everything. Forests and mountains, lakes and earth and tears and laughter. Whorls of time and humanity, and it all came down to this.

A Final Note

Three or four years ago, in the course of doing research for a different story, I came across a collection of mythological tales called "Nart Sagas." These stories originated in the Caucasus region and had been passed along by word of mouth for generations. In one of them, a warrior named Lepsch (sometimes Tlepsch) sets out to find the edge of the earth, convinced he will discover many things of importance there. But what he found was that everything he sought was his all along.

The story affected me deeply and resulted in this book. I owe a great debt of thanks to Dr. John Colarusso, whose book *Nart Sagas from the Caucasus* delves deeply into these sagas. While the story of the Adyghe document and its translation by Will and Charlotte is completely fictional, many of the mythological passages are excerpted (roughly) from Colarusso's translations of these ancient tales.

Around the same time, I became interested in the phenomenon of dying and extinct languages. This struck something in me as a writer and lover of language, and filled out the impetus of my love story here. After I had already finished writing Will and Charlotte's story, I was introduced by my friend Audrey to a documentary film called *The Linguists*, about two researchers who rove the planet in a quest to record dying languages, with all the danger and pathos that entails. I couldn't help but think of Ivo and Will, and of course, Charlotte. If you enjoyed this story, you might want to check it out.

One final point: The Republic of Adygea is a real place, but the town of Aleronsk and the local war that took place on these pages was completely made up. While there is a history of tension in the area, this book's events and characters were imagined for dramatic purposes only. To learn more about the Caucasus republics and their political and social histories, use a search engine or your library. It's a fascinating area to study.

About the Author

Molly Joseph loves to explore deep and complicated relationships on the pages of her books. She is also a multi-published BDSM romance author under the pen name Annabel Joseph.

You can find Molly's site and sign up for updates on upcoming books at www.mollyjosephnovels.com, or like her Facebook page at www.facebook.com/mollyjosephnovels. You can also find Molly on Twitter (@_MollyJoseph_).

Molly loves to hear from her readers at mollyjosephnovels@gmail.com.

An excerpt from *Cirque du Minuit*, a BDSM romance by Annabel Joseph, now available

The first knock was timid, a small *rap, rap* dragging his mind from the haze of sleep. Theo looked around, readjusting to wakefulness, seeking the source of the sound. It was dusk and he had to squint in the dim light. The next knock was louder and propelled him off the couch and to his feet. He swayed and reached for the side table to brace himself, knocking over a bottle of whiskey with a clank.

He winced and hunched toward the door. Theo didn't want to see anyone, didn't want anyone to see him. Again, *knock knock knock*, this time very loudly. He leaned to look through the peephole, making a concerted effort to recognize the long, light hair and blur of red lips.

"Theo?"

He stepped back. It was a woman, but he couldn't make her out from the tiny little spyglass set into the door. Melinde from Cirque headquarters again, or Diane. They had called and left message after message. Surely they didn't expect him to show up for work the day after—or had it been two days?

He looked at the clock. It was late. The evening's show would be over. Three days?

No, it was only the second day. What did they want from him? He leaned again to look through the peephole. She was still there, and she wasn't Diane or Melinde. The woman reached out to touch the door, then turned to rummage in the bag on her hip.

Theo stumbled back to the couch, taking a deep drink of whiskey right from the bottle to still the pounding in his head. It was so quiet. His little house was too warm, the air oppressive. He was sweating. *Go away. Just go away.*

He stared at the ceiling, willing the interloper to give up on whatever errand had brought her here. A moment later, a folded piece of paper slid under the door. He stared at it a long time before he moved.

He picked it up and turned on a light, but didn't open it. It was interaction, contact with another human being, which he wanted but didn't want at the same time. He set the folded paper on the side table and smoked three cigarettes in a row. He lit a fourth for courage and picked up the note, held the red, burning ashes to the edge of it. The paper curled and cringed in on itself. Light hair, red lips...

He put down the cigarette and tamped out the glimmering edge. He unfolded the smoldering note and stared through the haze of smoke at the messy but emphatic lettering.

Theo—
I'm so sorry about what happened. I hope you're okay. Everyone is worried about you.
Yesterday they skipped your act, and it was hard for everyone. They want to fill in for now with acrobatics or something. I don't know why I'm telling you that. I just don't know what to say. You don't even really know me, but I'm so sorry and I can't imagine how you feel. I wish there was something I could do.
If you need someone to talk to or you need anything, call me.

Below that, she'd signed her name, *Kelsey*, and scrawled a phone number. The digits swam before his eyes, as unfathomable as code. He lifted the cigarette and burned them off, every number, and then the rest of her message as well.

Two days later she was back again, knocking and calling his name through the door. He was less drunk, but still hot, too hot. He shook his head at her persistence and reeled into the bathroom. He turned the shower on cold and stood under the stream, shocked back to life, emerging from layers of misery back to reality.

Damn her. Blood rushed in his ears and he had to brace himself against the side of the shower to keep to his feet. He looked at the ceiling and yelled as loud as his lungs would let him, just because. Because he had to and because he didn't care. He yelled again, longer and harder until his lungs hurt, then shook his head and wiped the water from his eyes.

When he turned off the shower, he could still hear her. *Knock, knock, knock.* Didn't her knuckles hurt? He toweled off and pulled on some sweatpants, and slung the towel around his still-wet shoulders. *Knock, knock.* His hair was shaggy, overgrown. *Knock, knock.* It dripped cold water onto his shoulders as he stalked to the door and ripped it open.

White-blonde hair, red lips, and the realization in his brain like a set of gears clicking together. Of course. Her. That new acrobat who slid him looks when she thought he wasn't watching, her eyes glossy pools of curiosity and innocence at once. The one who'd stumbled in on him and Minya in the storeroom, and watched with that hungry gaze. The one person in the world he could least handle at the moment, with her cloying, immature adulation. He started to close the door, but she put one sneakered foot against it.

"I've been knocking for twenty minutes. Why didn't you answer?"

She was angry. Narrowed eyes, arms held tense at her side. He looked down his nose at her. "I was sleeping."

"You weren't sleeping." She gave a pointed look at his towel and dripping hair. "I heard you yelling. What were you yelling about?"

"I was yelling because someone keeps knocking on my door when I'm trying to sleep."

His tone and his expression, calculated to frighten, did not deter her at all. She pushed into his foyer, or maybe he let her in. She looked around the disarray of his living room. Empty whiskey bottles, scattered cigarette butts. A tangle of blankets on the couch, and the TV flickering in the corner, tuned to nothing. White noise. She turned those assessing eyes his way. He let her take him in, in all his hateful misery. *Still admire me now?* She looked at her feet and he almost felt sorry for her. Almost.

"What do you want? Why are you bothering me?" he snapped.

Her head came up, narrowed eyes again. Anger, a little fear. Pity. Sympathy. Guilt. The emotions played across her golden, prettily formed face like a mirror of all the things he felt. He fisted his hands and towered over her, trying to influence her back toward the door. She stood unmoving, setting her chin.

"Everyone's wondering where you are. Everyone's worried about whether you're okay."

"Everyone? Or you?"

She opened her mouth and closed it. "Are you okay?"

The question was ridiculous, and an answer impossible to frame. Was he okay? No. Was he going to discuss it with this scruffy, naïve little circus pervert? He frowned down at her. "I talked to Melinde yesterday on the phone. As you can see, I'm perfectly fine. If anyone is worried about me, this is their problem, not mine."

"If you're fine, why don't you come back? Why are you hiding in here and yelling in the shower?"

"I told you why I was yelling in the shower. And I'm hiding here precisely to avoid unwelcome confrontations like this one."

She let the words roll off her like water off some fluffy duck. "They're planning a memorial service for Minya. It's next Wednesday, after the show. You should come."

Dieu, she was so chipper. So indefatigable. A fluffy duck indeed. "You liked Minya, did you?" The way he asked it was intentionally sleazy and suggestive. She couldn't misunderstand. Now, finally, she inched back toward the door.

"We all miss her," she said quietly. "I'm sure you miss her most of all."

"You go away," he said, losing patience. "Go away, and don't come back here knocking any more. Because you saw me and Minya that day, you think now we are some kind of friends?" His English was fracturing, stymied by temper. She shook her head, big blue-pool eyes and blonde hair tilting over her shoulders, but he wasn't done. "You think you see that day, me and her, and now you know me? You know Minya? You know my grief and my problems? You can bother me and involve and tamper in my private life?"

"No. I just felt like— Look, that day—"

"You were wrong to do it, to spy," he said, pointing at her. "Do you even realize it?"

"Yes, I'm sorry. I'm sorry about that day. I would have apologized before but...it's awkward."

"You didn't have to watch."

The girl stared at her feet, toeing at the joints of the tiles. She was a baby. What, twenty years old? "I didn't know it bothered you so much," she said. "If you didn't want to be watched, why didn't you find someplace more private?"

"Like a dark storeroom?"

"Like your place, or hers." She waved a hand, backed almost to the door. "Look, I just wanted to be sure you were okay, that's all."

He sucked in a breath through his teeth, annoyed with himself for losing it. Annoyed with himself for trying to hurt her, for wanting to hurt her some more. "Go away," he said. "We're not friends. I'm not your thing to watch after. Not then, not now." He opened the door and nudged her through it. "Go away. This show is over for good."

Made in the USA
San Bernardino, CA
11 June 2016